# Zaedon's Kiss

## RAYNA TYLER

ISBN: 978-1-953213-02-0

# ALSO BY RAYNA TYLER

## Seneca Falls Shifters

Tempting the Wild Wolf
Captivated by the Cougar
Enchanting the Bear
Enticing the Wolf
Teasing the Tiger

## Ketaurran Warriors

Jardun's Embrace
Khyron's Claim
Zaedon's Kiss
Rygael's Reward
Logan's Allure
Garyck's Gift

## Crescent Canyon Shifters

Engaging His Mate
Impressing His Mate

## Bradshaw Bears

Bear Appeal

# CHAPTER ONE

*Cara*

Three weeks. That was all it had taken for Zaedon, the sexy ketaurran with a gorgeous smile and teasing personality, to get under my skin, to like him more than I should.

He made me want to punch him one minute and wrestle his clothes off the next. He was an elite warrior, a protector to the drezdarr—the planet's version of a ruler—and if ever there was a male I could fall for permanently, it would be him.

Too bad allowing myself to get close to any male wasn't something I could afford to do, not with the dangerous missions I undertook for Burke, the leader of the rebels who'd done his best to protect the humans during the Ketaurran War, and continued to work toward our survival afterward.

I liked my independence and volunteered because I'd seen too much death, suffered loss, and wanted to do my part to help, even if it meant putting my own life at risk.

My first encounter with Zaedon during the escape from the Quaddrien, a desolate area surrounded by rocky ledges the humans had nicknamed the wastelands, hadn't gone well, and since then, he'd gone out of his way to annoy me every chance he got.

The only reason he'd accompanied me to my grandparents' home in the farming community was because Khyron, the current drezdarr who'd brought an end to the war, had ordered him to be my personal bodyguard. Khyron, so unlike his uncle Sarus, the greedy, power-hungry male who'd caused the devastation in the first place, was intent on healing our world by uniting the humans and ketaurrans. It wasn't going to be an easy endeavor, not when a lot of the surviving humans had a strong dislike for his people.

To be fair, Khyron hadn't actually ordered Zaedon to come with me. He'd suggested with mild insistence, which amounted to the same thing. It hadn't helped that I now had a bounty on my head or that my friends Laria, Celeste, and Sloane enthusiastically agreed with Khyron's idea.

The bounty was courtesy of Doyle, a nasty mercenary whose sanity was highly questionable. I wasn't sure what had angered him more, the fact that I'd managed to infiltrate his compound disguised as a boy for nearly a month without detection, or that I'd destroyed his lab so he couldn't create any more of the deadly toxin he planned to use on the ketaurrans. Personally, I didn't think either action was a good enough reason to want me dead.

I refused to spend the rest of my life hiding or worrying that Doyle's males might eventually track me down to my grandparents' place. Finding a way to get rid of the bounty and keeping the remaining members of my family safe, hopefully without dying, was my main priority once the harvest I'd come home to help with was over. The last thing I needed was another complication, and Zaedon definitely qualified.

I heard the familiar sound of Zaedon's footsteps and knew he'd returned to the large building Josh used to house vehicles being repaired. "Ellie is a good cook," he said, not bothering with a greeting. "This pyteinna is quite delicious."

I could hear him chewing the flat cakes my grandmother had made from meat and a combination of plants. From my position underneath the harvester, all I could see were his boots and the lower end of his tail and knew he'd gone back to leaning against the vehicle's exterior. "You're not going to go away and stop hovering, are you?" I stared up at the metal underbelly, realizing I'd been so distracted by his presence earlier that I'd forgotten to grab the tool I needed to remove the metal plate covering the compartment housing the solars. It was a good thing, since I'd also forgotten to disconnect the power to the connectors inside the control panel.

Of the three harvesters, this machine had the most issues and broke down at least once during each of the four annual harvests. The plants my grandparents were in charge of growing fed everyone in the farming community as well as the nearby settlement where Burke and my friends lived. Since the plants would be ready to pick in a day or two, I'd decided to test the solar engine ahead of time to make sure we didn't have any problems.

Josh, one of a handful of engineers who'd been part of the *Starward Bounty*'s exploration team before the ship had crashed on Ketaurrios and stranded all of us here, was responsible for building the machines. In his midtwenties, he was bright for his age and always trying to devise ways to make life for the community residents easier.

Even though the planet's inhabitants didn't have the technology required to create a state-of-the-art harvester like the ones back on Earth, Josh had done a decent job with whatever he could find to build them. Normally, he'd be doing the maintenance, but he'd been working on one of his many projects and broken two fingers on one hand. Besides being good at covert missions, I was also a darned good mechanic and had offered him my help.

"You do not expect me to disobey the drezdarr's order,

do you?" I heard the smugness in Zaedon's voice and imagined the grin on his face.

"You know he didn't exactly *order* you to come with me."

"Maybe not, but I made a promise to Laria, Celeste, and Sloane that I would assist with your safety, and I am honor-bound to comply with their wishes."

It was the same excuse he'd used the last two times I suggested he return to the settlement. I'd been around the vryndarr long enough to know honor and integrity were highly valued. There was no way I could argue with his excuse, not without insulting him.

Before Zaedon and I left the settlement, I didn't get a chance to ask my friends why they'd thought having him accompany me was such a good idea. Having a lengthy discussion with them was at the top of my list of things to do the next time I saw them.

Trying to keep my mind focused on the task and not filled with images of Zaedon's broad chest covered with blue scales, his piercing turquoise eyes, and a tail that begged to be caressed got harder with each passing day. Especially when the tail I was trying to ignore kept finding its way under the vehicle and was currently rubbing against my leg.

I grabbed the tip, the scales a lot smoother than I'd expected. "Lose something?" When I shook his tail, he moaned. My grip wasn't tight, so I didn't think I'd really caused him any pain.

"Cara." His voice came out raspy and deeper than usual. "You should not…" He jerked his tail out of my hand.

"I shouldn't what?" I scooted the roller, a long rectangular sheet of wood with small wheels on each side, out from under the harvester.

"Nothing." He turned, giving me his back, suddenly taking an interest in the tools spread out on a nearby bench.

I frowned when he wouldn't look at me. "If I hurt your tail, I'm sorry."

"You did not." He blew out a sigh, then turned to face me, offering a hand and pulling me to my feet.

"A male's tail is sensitive, but it is extremely responsive to a female's touch." He moved closer, the space between us mere inches. "And when you…"

It took me only a second to realize that grabbing his tail had caused pleasure, not pain. "Oh."

He grinned wickedly. "I did not mind, nor would I be opposed if you wished to touch it again." He curled his tail around the backs of my legs.

This was the first time he'd openly made it known the attraction I'd been experiencing wasn't one-sided. Not that it mattered, I wasn't going to change my mind about getting involved with him. I'd been down that path before, gotten close to Graham, and he'd ended up dead, killed during one of our missions.

His death had nearly destroyed me, and I'd vowed I'd never let another male get that close to me again. "No, I'm good." Unwilling to touch his tail again, I let my gaze drift downward, signaling him to remove it from my legs.

With a disappointed sigh, he dropped his tail to the floor. "If you should decide otherwise…" The rest of his insinuation remained unsaid. He studied me for several more uncomfortable seconds, then asked, "Have you completed your maintenance already?"

I was thankful for the subject change. "No, I need to undo the connectors first." He'd also been semi-assisting me with repairs, knew that I always disconnected the power supply before starting any work. I didn't want him questioning me about the reason I hadn't done it before getting underneath the harvester. I pointed at the tools spread out on the bench behind him. "Would you mind handing me that screwdriver?"

Luckily, I was one of the few people Josh entrusted to use the handful of tools he'd salvaged from the crash.

"It is the one with the red handle, correct?"

Zaedon might hide his intelligence behind a charming smile, but he'd been paying attention to everything I did during the few weeks he'd spent shadowing me. I hid my grin. "Yes, that's the one." I removed the side panel covering the main controls.

He stood behind me and leaned closer, his taller, broader frame a comfortable fit, not a suffocating invasion of my personal boundaries.

"This connection looks different from the ones on the other vehicles." His breath gently caressed my neck, his body warming my back and distracting me further.

I forced my attention back to the unit, noting the slight change in the configuration. "I wonder if Josh made another modification without telling me."

"It will still need to be disconnected for you to work on the solars, correct?" Zaedon asked.

"Yes, but I need…" I reacted too slowly to stop him from touching the connector with the screwdriver's tip.

I saw the spark, knew the current had jumped between the two metals. With a grunt, Zaedon dropped the tool and stepped backward. His foot caught the edge of the roller, the wheels spun, the board moved forward, and he lost his footing. The flailing aerial display he made might have been humorous if he hadn't hit the ground hard, then lain there with his eyes closed, unmoving.

My heart lurched, and I rushed to his side, gripping his cheeks as I knelt over him. "Zaedon, please tell me you're okay?"

His body was so still, I couldn't tell if he was breathing. Ketaurrans resembled humans in many ways, but I had no idea how to test one for a pulse. Fortunately, I'd learned CPR before I left Earth. I hadn't used the skill in a long time, but remembered the basics. As soon as I reached the part where I placed my mouth over his, Zaedon's strong arms wrapped around my waist. My attempt at saving his life turned into a breath-stealing kiss, which ended with me sprawled on top of him and my arms braced on either side of his head.

He grinned, his turquoise eyes sparkling with amusement. "Were you worried about me, Cara?"

I was relieved and irritated at the same time. "Of all the arrogant... You're not hurt, are you?" I smacked his chest, then tried to roll away and ended up on my back with him straddling me. I'd learned plenty of combat maneuvers from Burke's guys and could have easily removed Zaedon, but chose to see what he planned to do next.

"Vryndarr do not wound easily." He smirked.

"So why did you let me think you were... And why did you kiss me?"

He leaned closer, his cheek close to mine, then inhaled a deep breath. "I assumed it was your wish since you placed your mouth on mine."

"I was giving you mouth-to-mouth."

"Exactly, which is why I complied."

I smacked his shoulder. "No, you don't understand. Mouth-to-mouth is what humans do to help someone who has stopped breathing."

"My breathing is fine, but if you think I require more assistance"—Zaedon lowered his mouth closer to mine— "I would be happy to oblige you."

Thinking about the kiss we'd just shared, and the possibility of doing it again, had my body heating all over. The temptation was interrupted by the sound of a creak as someone opened the wooden door on the opposite side of the building.

"Derrick, I'm pretty sure Cara's in here somewhere. She told me she planned to spend the day working on the harvester."

The jolt of embarrassment I got from hearing my grandmother's voice, then realizing she wasn't alone, was enough to chill the moment and make me squirm.

Ellie had been after me for quite some time to move on and find another male. She'd be thrilled to find Zaedon and me tangled together on the floor. Somehow, the irritating male had charmed her to the point of adoration. She went out of her way to make Zaedon feel welcome and had insisted he use one of the spare rooms in our house instead of staying in the visitor building.

Derrick was another matter. His resentment toward the ketaurrans had gotten worse during the war, and he didn't have a problem sharing his negative views with anyone who'd listen. He'd been Graham's friend, and though he'd never given me a reason to personally dislike him, there was something about him that triggered my distrust.

Not long after Graham's death, he'd started hanging around more often, showing more than a friendly interest. An interest I discouraged, almost to the point of avoiding him. After the few times I'd noticed him giving Zaedon disapproving glares when he thought I wasn't looking, I figured it was best not to give Derrick a reason to go after him.

I pushed against Zaedon's chest. "You need to get off."

He didn't budge. "But why?" He feigned ignorance with a quirk of his brow, but his tone held a note of mischief. In all the time he'd been here, I'd never seen Zaedon act disrespectful or unpleasant to anyone living in the community. Only someone who'd been paying close attention, like me, would have noticed that the animosity between Derrick and Zaedon was mutual.

I grabbed the tip of his tail, and instead of playfully shaking it, I squeezed hard.

Zaedon snarled and rolled to the side, pulling his tail out of my reach. "You do not play fair." He held out his hand, helping me to my feet seconds before Derrick and Ellie appeared around the corner of the harvester.

"Everything okay out here?" Ellie noticed Zaedon holding my hand and smiled.

I slipped my hand from his and moved to lean against the bench. "Everything is fine. Why?" My grandparents weren't what anyone would call typical and had never been big on following social standards, even when we lived on Earth. They believed they were a lot younger than they were and insisted I call them by their first names.

Ellie answered by running her hand along the side of my head and smoothing some of my short wild curls. Curls I'd inherited from her side of the family. Only her long brown strands were a few shades lighter, sprinkled with silver, and were kept pulled back in a tie during the day while she worked. "I still don't understand why you cut your hair. It was so beautiful when it was long."

My grandmother knew I worked with Burke but assumed all I did was acquire supplies. She spent enough time worrying about me and didn't need to know how dangerous my job could be, or that I'd cut my hair to look like a boy so I could infiltrate a mercenary's compound.

I hated the shorter length. It was hard to manage, and I couldn't wait for it to get longer. "Thought I'd try something different." I shrugged, glancing at the container she was carrying. "What's in there?"

"I had some pyteinna left over and thought you might like them." Ellie walked over to Zaedon and handed him the container she'd been carrying.

Zaedon inclined his head. "Thank you. That was very thoughtful."

Ellie's cheeks flushed at the compliment. I rolled my eyes, doubtful that the flat cakes Zaedon clutched like a coveted prize to his chest were left over since I'd heard him munching on one not too long ago. Ellie wouldn't admit it, but she'd probably made a new batch especially for him.

Derrick must have come to the same conclusion, because his forced smile turned into a sneer. When he opened his mouth to say what I was sure would be a snide comment, I cut him off. "Derrick, did you need something?"

\*\*\*

*Zaedon*

Kissing Cara had been even more intoxicating than I had imagined. Even now, my lips tingled with the aftereffects. Had we not been interrupted, I was certain I could have coaxed her into another taste of her soft, full lips. If she had not insisted I help her off the floor, I would have remained where we were so that Derrick, the human male who'd accompanied Ellie, could see us. Maybe then he'd lose interest in Cara and stop interfering with my plans to win her over, to finally tell her she was my ketiorra.

Not only was he annoying, there was something about the male that made my scales itch. It was an unpleasant feeling, a warning of sorts. And if I was a luzardee, I would have shed my skin two or three times already.

For a human, Derrick's lean frame lacked the height and muscular build I had noticed in most of the males who worked with Burke. He did not hide the fact that he disliked ketaurrans. I had seen the expression often enough on the face of other humans. It was the guarded glares of hatred, the ones he shielded from Cara and her family that made me wary. Similar to the one he quickly masked soon after his dark gaze landed on me.

Derrick ignored Cara's question regarding his needs and countered with one of his own. "What's he still doing here? I would have thought he'd be bored with our village and left by now."

As a vryndarr, my travels had taken me to many places, but I had never visited any of the human farming communities. The one where Cara resided when she was not working with Burke resembled a small village surrounded on three sides by large lush fields filled with deep-burgundy-colored plants. The ground beyond the fields gradually turned into sandy dirt sprinkled with huge boulders, and, in some areas along the perimeter, they formed tall walls of rock.

Including Ellie and Isaac, Cara's grandparents, there were five other families, couples with children, who'd started the community after their spaceship had crash-landed on Ketaurrios. The families lived in their own dwellings, and the single residents, or occasional visitors, stayed in one of several dorm-like buildings.

"I find *Cara's home* quite enjoyable." I gripped the container Ellie had given me tighter. "I will be staying until the drezdarr orders me otherwise." Even if Khyron had not suggested I accompany Cara to ensure her safety after learning about Doyle's bounty, I would not have let her leave the human settlement without me.

Luckily, her friends Laria, Celeste, and Sloane had come to my aid and eagerly insisted I go with her. Cara was an excellent fighter and quite skilled at taking care of herself. At first, she had been angry about my presence and did her best to avoid me. Eventually, her attitude changed. Even the banter we shared regarding the situation had gone from tense to almost playful.

"Okay, then." Cara moved closer to Ellie, putting her directly between us.

I could fend for myself, did not need her help defending me from the puny male. Had she been any other female, I would have found the protective act insulting, not be exhilarated with the hope that she cared about my well-being.

"Was there something you needed, Derrick?" Cara asked again.

Disappointed by Cara's lack of support, Derrick slumped his shoulders. "Yeah, I'm helping Josh with one of his projects, and he sent me to get some tools." He kept his distance from me and shuffled to the opposite end of the long work bench. After selecting the two he needed, he started to leave, pausing to glance back at Cara. "Guess I'll see you later."

She gave him a reluctant nod, then turned to Ellie. "So,

is everything on track for the harvest?"

"Isaac is meeting with the other families to assign tasks, and, so far, no problems." Ellie peered through the opening where Cara had removed the panel on the harvester. "How's the maintenance going?"

"Not sure yet." Cara frowned. "We had a problem with one of the parts, and I need to take a closer look at it."

"I'm sure you'll have it running in no time, so I'll let you two get back to it." Ellie winked at me on her way out of the building.

As soon as the door creaked shut, Cara said, "I'm sorry about Derrick. He's…"

"Not your responsibility." I tweaked her chin. "He is nothing more than a bite to my backside."

Cara giggled. "I think the phrase you're looking for is 'pain in the ass,' but your version works fine too."

She snatched a pyteinna out of the container before I could move it out of her reach. "Come on, let's get back to work." She quickly ate the flat cake, then grabbed an extraction tool off the bench.

I stared at her back while she removed the defective part, pondering a question I had considered asking her more than once. "Cara."

"Yeah." She gave the tool one last twist, freeing the part.

"Why do you not tell Ellie and Isaac the truth?"

She turned, concern marring her features. "The truth about what?"

"About what happened with Doyle? Do you not think you should tell them about the bounty?" I asked.

"No, and you aren't going to tell them either." She sighed, flipping a loose curl off her face. "They don't know about the work I really do for Burke, and I'd like to keep it that way."

I placed the container on the bench, then leaned against the edge. "What explanation do you give them when you are gone for long periods of time?"

"They think I go to the settlement to work with my friends, or possibly to spend time with a male."

The thought of Cara with another male was almost my undoing. I crossed my arms to keep from clenching my fists, but failed to keep my tail from swishing and banging against a corner leg of the bench. "Is there a male?" It was difficult to ask the question without growling.

"No, that's what Ellie assumes, and I don't bother correcting her." Her perceptive gaze dropped to my tail, then back to my face. "Actually, I avoid those kind of relationships."

Her admission was not going to make my task of getting close to her any easier, but it was a relief to know I would not have to hurt another male to remove any competition.

*\*\*\**

*Cara*

"I see." Zaedon's response to my comment about not getting involved with a male in a relationship baffled me. I wasn't sure what he saw, but his tone suggested he'd uncovered a hidden secret.

I gave him a curious glance, then went back to examining the part by viewing it from different angles. "This isn't good."

"What is wrong?" He pushed away from the bench, moving closer to see what I was talking about.

"There's a lot of damage." I turned the part to show him the blackened area around the connectors. "Are you sure you didn't do this on purpose so you could stay here longer?"

He ran a hand roughly through the cinnamon streaks in his dark hair. "Cara, you have to know that I would never purposely…"

I placed my hand on his arm. "Zaedon, I was teasing. I

know it was an accident." I shook my head. "We do have a problem, though."

The hint of relief I'd seen in his eyes disappeared. "Which is?"

"This part is ruined, and the only person who can repair it lives in Golyndier, a town not far from here."

"But I thought you could repair anything."

I returned the extraction tool to its place on the bench. "Repair, yes. Reconstruct, no."

"What about Josh? Can he not fix it?" Zaedon asked.

"Not with broken fingers. And even if he could, we don't have the parts to replace the damaged area on the connectors."

"I am opposed to the idea of leaving. It will put your life at greater risk."

If he thought he could intimidate me by crossing his arms and flexing his muscles, he was wrong. I dropped the part on the bench, then stepped in front of him with my hands on my hips. "This is not about me."

I hadn't lied when I told Zaedon there was only one person I knew of who could repair the part, but it wasn't the only reason I wanted to go to Golyndier. Besides wanting to see Torrlun and his family, thinking about an extended stay in the community made me restless. I needed to get back to work, to help Khyron's new collaboration team, of which I was a member, find out who was trying to kill him and possibly start another war.

I couldn't do anything to help if I was stuck out here wondering how much longer I could keep my whereabouts hidden. Doyle would never give up. It was only a matter of time before he discovered where I was and sent someone after me. If mercs showed up in the community, people I cared about would get hurt, or worse. Thinking about the possibilities caused me more than one night of restless sleep.

Having the bounty disappear was the only way to resolve the situation. In order to make that happen, I needed more information. Getting the part repaired provided the perfect opportunity. Not only could I visit my friends, but I could contact one of my sources and find out what I wanted to know.

I knew if I told Zaedon what I had in mind, he'd strongly disagree, maybe even send word to Khyron in an attempt to stop me. It would be a lot easier dealing with Zaedon, slipping away from him if necessary, than it would be if I had all my friends watching my every move.

"Cara, please." He softened his tone, trying a different tact when I wouldn't back down.

I didn't want to fight with him, but this was a battle of wills I needed to win. "No, you don't understand. A lot of people rely on the harvest to survive. Without those plants, they won't have enough food to make it until the next season. I need to get the harvester up and running. So you can either come with me or stay here. Your choice."

# CHAPTER TWO

*Zaedon*

I stared out the viewing pane above the control panel of the solarveyor at the sandy dirt road and bordering rock formations. Tension rippled through my body, and I strained to keep a smile on my lips. Even though Vince, one of Burke's males, had visited a week earlier and stated that no one had heard anything new about the bounty Doyle had placed on Cara, I was not happy about traveling to Golyndier. The overwhelming need to keep Cara safe was a constant struggle.

I had made an oath long ago to the old drezdarr, Khyron's father, that I would protect all humans. After learning that many would starve if the harvester was not repaired, I could not argue against Cara's insistence about making the trip, but there was no way I would allow her to travel alone.

Times after the war were difficult, survival a lot harder. Experience had taught me that not all beings, which sometimes included friends, could be trusted, that the offer of additional cradassons was a temptation some could not resist. I had been concerned that someone might recognize Cara's vehicle and report her presence to one of the mercs searching for her.

Since Cara had completed the repairs to Laria's solarveyor, the one her friend treasured and had followed a human custom by naming Trixie, I suggested using the vehicle to make the trip. It was the first time the frustrating female agreed with me.

When she offered to drive, I didn't argue, preferring to take the seat next to her. It enabled me to keep a close watch on our surroundings and steal an occasional glimpse of her.

"You know this trip would be a lot more fun if you weren't planning on being mad at me the whole time." Cara shot an annoyed glance in my direction, then tucked a strand of hair behind her ear.

Yesterday was not the first time Ellie had mentioned the length of Cara's hair. Imagining what she'd looked like with longer chestnut curls draped loosely over her shoulders had entertained my thoughts numerous times.

The state of her hair was not the only thing I fantasized about. Having her in my bed and exploring her beautiful body had filled many of my dreams. From the moment I sniffed her alluring scent once she had cleaned the dirt from her body after our mission in the Quaddrien, I knew she was my ketiorra and could think of nothing else.

Besides being a skilled warrior, with or without a weapon, she was the most difficult human female I had ever met. So far, any attempt I had made to get close to her ended in failure. Though having her respond so willingly to my kiss gave me hope that I would eventually make some progress.

"What makes you believe I am upset?" I was, but I thought I had done a better job of hiding my frustration.

"Oh, I don't know, maybe because you haven't said or done anything to irritate me since we left the farm." She teased with a grin.

It was not at all what I expected her to say and could

not help but laugh. "I am certain I can find many ways to improve the situation."

"Of that I have no doubt." She adjusted the controls, slowing the vehicle. "I guess irritating me will have to wait. We're almost there."

Returning my gaze to the pane, I could see the shape of buildings taking form in the distance. When we reached the edge of the small city, Cara veered to the right, taking a road that skirted the perimeter and led to a large area where other solarveyors in various sizes were parked.

"Most of these belong to visitors who come to trade in the market," Cara said.

Several of the larger cities and most of the smaller towns in the area had trader markets. Many craftsman and farmers, human and ketaurran alike, who didn't mind traveling, ventured among the handful of settlements, selling or trading their wares.

After parking between two larger vehicles, making it difficult to see our transport from a distance, Cara slipped out of her seat and reached for her hooded jacket. "It will be easier to blend in if we walk from here."

I noticed her putting on the coat without securing a belt and knife to her hip as I had. "Are you not taking a blade?"

"I don't need one." She flexed her fingers. "I'm already armed."

"I have grown so used to seeing Laria, Celeste, and Sloane wield their blades that I forgot you prefer to use your body as a weapon." Thinking about her firm muscles had my body heating and my shaft hardening. I could not afford the distraction, nor did I want Cara to notice how much her nearness affected me.

I quickly donned my coat. It was similar to Cara's, but in a darker shade of brown. The thigh-length worked well for concealing weapons and the hood kept me from being easily recognized.

She chuckled. "There are times when not being armed

works in my favor." She strapped a bag containing the part over her shoulder and opened the access door. "You ready?"

I nodded, then followed her outside. Shortly after passing several buildings, Cara placed her hand on my arm, stopping me before we reached the open area designated for selling. "I think we should avoid the market." She tipped her head toward a narrow walkway between two buildings on the left. "This way."

I remained silent, letting her lead, warily surveying our surroundings and noting anything I could use as a landmark later. We took three different walkways before reaching a long stretch of dirt wide enough to accommodate a transport.

Cara glanced in my direction. "It's the dwelling on the end."

Most of the buildings we passed were constructed from wood, the exteriors sealed with a sandy mixture to protect them from the ever-changing weather. This one appeared to be well maintained, the cracks in the protective layer less noticeable than on the home sitting next to it.

The knock Cara had given the door was answered in less than a minute. I had expected a human to answer, not the older ketaurran male with dark hair and light blue scales.

"Surprise," Cara said, pushing the hood from her head.

The male grinned, his dark amber eyes widening. "Cara." The male pulled her into a hug and lifted her off her feet. "It has been a long time."

"Too long." She stepped back with a giggle after he returned her feet to the ground.

Jealousy was not something I had experienced often, at least not until I met Cara. Witnessing their comfortable familiarity sparked the emotion, forcing me to disguise a possessive growl with a cough.

Cara pinned me with a narrow-eyed glare. "Zaedon, this is Torrlun, the mechanical expert I was telling you about."

"Cara notoriously exaggerates my skills." He hid the perusal he gave me behind a charming smile. "Please come in." He stepped aside, motioning for us to enter. "Erin and Rajak will be excited to see you."

Cara expectantly glanced around the large room he led us through. The center area was clear, leaving an open pathway to the opposite side of the room. A dining table and chairs sat off to the right, and two small loungers were positioned near the wall on the left. Everything in the room appeared to be neat and clean, reflecting the same kind of care as the exterior of the building.

"They have gone to the market and will be back shortly," Torrlun said as he walked into another room resembling a much smaller version of the building Cara and Josh used for repairs. Workbenches lined two of the walls, one of them displaying a wide selection of tools. Although their design was similar to the tools Josh brought from Earth, it was obvious they were crafted by a ketaurran.

Torrlun turned and leaned against one of the benches, bracing his hands along the edge. "Since you brought a guest, I assume there is a reason for your visit."

"I need your expertise." Cara reached into the bag strapped to her shoulder, pulled out the damaged unit, and handed it to Torrlun.

"This part is from the power unit on one of the harvesters. It was accidentally damaged and I need to know how quickly you can repair it."

Torrlun held the piece at eye level. After he'd examined it from various angles, the furrow between his brows deepened. "This was not caused by an accident."

"Are you certain?" I shared a glance with Cara, relieved that my eagerness to assist her the day before had not caused the damage.

"Quite certain." Torrlun held up the part, waiting for us to move closer, then pointed at a gap between the connectors. "It has been tampered with. See the tiny scrapes in the metal?"

"Huh." Cara squinted. "They're barely noticeable."

"If the harvester had been fully operational, the changes made to this part might have destroyed the solars."

"And you believe that why?" Cara asked, skepticism in her tone.

"If you look closely, there is also a difference in this connector compared to the one next to it."

"Yeah, Zaedon pointed that out right before he touched it with a screwdriver."

"I assume you received quite a shock." Torrlun directed his comment at me.

I nodded, remembering the brief jolt of pain that ended with Cara's wonderful kiss.

"Cara, has anyone else been working on the harvester?" Torrlun asked.

"No. Josh broke a couple of fingers, so it's only been Zaedon and me." She adjusted the strap on her bag. "Why?"

Torrlun pursed his lips. "Because it is possible that the person responsible for altering the part meant to disable the harvester."

\*\*\*

*Cara*

Zaedon didn't need to say anything for me to know Torrlun's comment about the part troubled him. The stiffness in his shoulders and tightly clamped jaw was a good indication he believed the sabotage to the harvester had something to do with me. I didn't believe in coincidences and hoped this was one of those rare occasions when I was wrong.

The possibility that someone from the farming

community knew about Doyle's bounty and figured out I was the person he was after were slim. Not everyone who lived in the village had been there for years. People came, stayed for a few months, decided it wasn't the kind of life they wanted, then left. Since I didn't live there on a full-time basis, I didn't get a chance to really get to know any of the newcomers.

What bothered me most was the connection to the harvester. If someone was targeting me, did they know I'd seek outside help in order to keep the vehicle running? And if they did, what else had they done to make sure they collected a payment?

"I don't get it. What would anyone gain by damaging the harvester?" I hoped by steering Zaedon's concerns in another direction, he wouldn't think he had a good reason to cut our trip short before I could accomplish my other task.

Zaedon pinned me with a perceptive glare. "Perhaps it was not the machine they were after."

I knew he took his job as my bodyguard seriously, but in the last few days, I'd noticed something more to his overprotective behavior. There was passion involved in the kiss he'd given me yesterday. A passion I'd been determined to avoid after Graham died. A passion I'd had no problem sharing.

Zaedon had a way of drawing out my emotions, the ones I tried to keep restrained, and before I could stop myself, I placed a comforting hand on his arm. "We don't know that for sure."

"Is there something I should know?" Torrlun's gaze jumped from Zaedon to me.

"Nope, nothing." I moved a little closer to Zaedon, ready to elbow him in the ribs if he decided to discuss his suspicions with Torrlun any further. Luckily, the sound of a door closing and the rapid pounding of little footsteps ended the conversation.

"Cara." Torrlun's son, Rajak, squealed as he raced into

the room. I barely had time to turn before the five-year-old child launched himself into my arms. He'd gotten his blond curls and blue eyes from his human mother. The defined cheekbones and pale green scales covering his chest and tail were Torrlun's contribution to his creation.

"Rajak." I spun around a couple of times, then nuzzled the ticklish spot on his neck, enjoying the giggles that filled the room.

"Did you bring me something?" He didn't wait for an answer before sticking his small hand in my jacket pocket.

"Rajak, what did I tell you?" Erin appeared in the doorway, adjusting the tote bag hooked over her shoulder, and rubbing her protruding belly. The sparkling amusement in her blue eyes didn't match the sternness in her voice.

He pushed out his lower lip, then twisted in my arms to face his mother. "Not to expect gifts from visitors."

I snorted, then winked at Rajak. "But I'm not a visitor. I'm family, so it doesn't count." I set him on the floor, then reached inside my bag and pulled out a small container filled with tiny red balls, the ketaurran version of candy, and handed it to him.

"Thanks, Cara." He wrapped his small arms around my leg, his tail swishing rapidly. He turned and ran from the room, squealing even louder than he had before.

Erin shook her head as she watched her child's departure. "You know he'll be impossible to deal with the rest of the day."

"Yes, but he's so cute, it's worth it." I walked over to Erin, leaning forward to give her a hug, being careful not to press against her midsection. "You've gotten a lot bigger." Several months had passed since I'd last visited. At the time, Erin had just found out she was going to have another child.

"Don't remind me." She flashed Torrlun a loving smile. "He's convinced it's going to be a female."

Torrlun walked over and pressed a kiss to Erin's

forehead. "One who will be as beautiful as her dam." He took a step back, then turned to Zaedon, who'd remained near the bench watching the exchange, amusement glinting in his turquoise eyes. "Zaedon, this is my ketiorra, Erin."

Zaedon grinned, tipping his head. "It is a pleasure to meet you."

During all the excitement, Rajak must not have noticed Zaedon. No sooner had Zaedon started talking than Rajak returned, squeezing his way past the door frame and his mother's leg to stand in front of her. "Mama, who is that male?" He pointed and glared at Zaedon.

It seemed being protective of females started at a young age for ketaurran males.

Zaedon crouched so he was eye level with Rajak and less imposing. "I am Zaedon, a friend of Cara's."

"Is that true?" Rajak tipped his head back, looking at me for confirmation.

"Yes, fierce little warrior." I tweaked his nose.

Rajak smiled. "Okay."

Erin held out her hand to Rajak. "Why don't we go find something to play with and let them finish discussing their business?"

"Can we play with the new blocks we got at the market?"

"New blocks it is. Come on." Erin took his hand and let him lead her into the adjoining room.

Once Erin and Rajak were gone, I asked Torrlun, "How long will it take you to repair the part?"

Torrlun scratched his jaw. "Should I presume this is one of your rush jobs?"

"You should," I said.

"I will need several hours. Zaedon can assist me if you want to go spend time with Erin and help her calm Rajak."

"I suppose if you don't want to stay and help Torrlun, you can always check out Rajak's new blocks," I teased Zaedon.

"Go, enjoy your time with the young one. I am certain

I will be fine in here."

Things were falling into place. With Zaedon preoccupied, it would make what I planned to do a lot easier. Yet when I walked into the other room, I couldn't help feeling a little guilty about deceiving him.

"Cara, you have to sit here and watch." Rajak patted the floor beside a large pillow next to him.

"Sorry, he insisted that we sit on the floor and watch him build things with his blocks." Erin had already taken a seat on another pillow and was resting her back against the front of a lounger.

"Not a problem." I removed my bag, setting it off to the side, then plopped in the middle of the pillow, sitting cross-legged. Facing Torrlun's workshop, I could see the males conversing and had a good view of Zaedon and his well-toned backside. Whenever we were together, he was usually too busy hovering, so it was nice to be able to observe him from a distance.

I picked up one of Rajak's wooden blocks, noting the accuracy of the square design. "Someone put a lot of effort into carving these."

"The male who makes these shows up every couple of months with something new. He doesn't have a problem with bartering, so I can usually get whatever I want by trading a container or two of flat cakes."

"Rajak's grown quite a bit since the last time I was here too." I handed the block to the child, which immediately found a place on the wall he was building.

"I know." Erin playfully tousled the hair on the top of his head, earning her an irritated swipe from her child. She repositioned herself on the pillow, then smiled. "So, tell me all about your new male." She tipped her head toward the other room. "He's rather handsome."

Handsome didn't even come close to describing how hot I thought Zaedon was, or how much I'd miss not having him around. I was about to betray his trust, which would definitely push him away and made me feel even worse.

"He's not my new anything. We just work together."

"Uh-huh."

"Stop giving me that look. I know what you're thinking, and you're wrong." Like Laria, Erin had an extraordinary gift for perception and could always see the things I didn't want anyone else to know.

"If you say so." Her grin irritated me even more.

With a groan, I picked up another block and handed it to Rajak.

"Can you at least tell me how you met?"

Torrlun and Erin knew I worked for Burke, but they had no idea how dangerous some of my missions could be. For their own safety, I wanted to keep it that way and needed to be careful what I told her. She'd met some of my friends from the settlement. I hoped giving her a partial truth would satisfy her inquiry.

"I met him while I was doing some work with Laria, Celeste, and Sloane." I left out the part about rescuing Vurell, Khyron's physician, and stealing the toxin designed to kill ketaurrans along with its antidote. I also didn't mention how Zaedon refused to leave my side when I stayed behind to hold off Doyle's males, giving the rest of the group time to reach the solarveyor. Even then, after barely knowing me for five minutes, he'd risked his life to help me.

I held up my hand when it looked like she was going to ask another question. "That's all I can tell you."

"Fair enough," Erin said.

She and I had an understanding. If I let her know there were details I couldn't divulge, she wouldn't press for more information. Thinking about Zaedon and our escape from the Quaddrien reminded me that I had questions of my own. Questions I didn't feel comfortable asking him directly, at least not yet, but I could ask Erin.

She'd gotten together with Torrlun not long after we arrived on Ketaurrios. If anyone had insight into a ketaurran male's behavior, it would be her. "There is something I've noticed, one thing I'm curious about."

She chuckled. "Only one?"

I puffed out an exasperated sigh. "Does being more difficult have anything to do with being pregnant?"

"I have always been difficult."

"That's true." I laughed.

"What did you want to know?" Erin asked.

"I've noticed that Zaedon sniffs me a lot. Is that normal? Do I smell funny?"

Rajak raised his head and inhaled a deep breath. "You don't smell funny to me." He'd been so quiet, appearing to be concentrating on his new creation, that I'd forgotten he liked to listen to everything the adults around him were saying. He didn't understand boundaries and had no problem repeating what he'd heard, blurting comments at inopportune moments that usually caused considerable embarrassment.

"Thanks." I leaned forward and kissed his forehead. I looked at Erin, noting her amused grin. "You know why, but you're not going to tell me, are you?"

Her gaze filled with empathy. "I do, but it's something you need to discuss with Zaedon."

Yeah, I could already see how that conversation would go. There was no way I was going to ask him why he had a problem with my scent. Zaedon's first comment after we'd met was to compare my smell to chaugwas dung. At first, I thought the sniffing thing had to do with the grime I'd used to cover my body to keep Doyle's males from discovering I wasn't a boy.

Many of the males had no respect for females, and if they'd uncovered my true identity, I would have been forced from one bed to another. Or worse, traded into slavery in one of the secluded outlying areas that most humans avoided.

Even after several showers of thoroughly scrubbing myself, the sniffing had continued. Maybe not to the degree of our first meeting, but it was still noticeable.

After another twenty minutes of catching up and hearing about things going on in the town, I decided it was time to make my escape. "I need to run an errand."

"Okay." Erin started to get up, and I placed my hand on her arm to stop her.

"Things with Zaedon are complicated, and I can't take him with me." I didn't want to put Erin in the middle, but I needed her to cover for me. "I hate to ask, but can you stay here with Rajak and not mention that I left?"

"You cannot leave. You just got here." Rajak sat back on his haunches and crossed his arms, reminding me a lot of Torrlun. "Where are you going, anyway?"

I tapped his cute little nose. "It's a secret, but I promise I won't be gone long, okay?"

"Okay." He shrugged, then went back to stacking his blocks.

"I've seen the way Zaedon watches you." Erin kept her voice low. "It won't take long after you leave for him to notice." She squeezed my hand. "And when he does, he won't be happy that you didn't talk to him first."

I knew Zaedon would be angry, but would he be furious enough to ask Khyron to replace him with someone else. Up until now, I hadn't realized how much it would bother me if he left, and I came close to changing my mind. But altering my plans now wasn't going to make Doyle's threat go away or keep my family safe.

"I know, and I'll deal with it when I get back." I returned her squeeze. "All I need is a few minutes' head start."

Erin glanced toward the workshop as she spoke. "Then go, be quick and be careful."

"I will, I promise." I slowly scooted across the floor, dragging my bag along with me. As soon as I was out of Zaedon's line of sight, I jumped to my feet and raced for the door.

# CHAPTER THREE

*Zaedon*

After the intense perusal Torrlun had given me when Cara and I first arrived, I was certain an interrogation of sorts was the real reason he had asked me to remain behind in his workshop. He waited until the females were out of hearing distance and settled in the adjoining room with Rajak before speaking.

"Cara usually travels alone. It has been a long time since she…" He dismissed whatever he was going to say with a wave of his hand.

I was more than a little curious to hear what Cara hadn't done in a long time, but figured by his refusal to share that it must be something she needed to tell me herself.

After setting the damaged part on the bench in front of him, he shifted his gaze back to me. "Should I be worried that one of the drezdarr's warriors accompanies her now?"

Vryndarr were trained to hide the true nature of their identities. I had done nothing I was aware of to expose my abilities and wondered how he had deduced my status. Pretending I had no idea what he was talking about would be an insult. "How did you know?"

"During the war, I had the honor of assisting several vryndarr when they attempted to help the humans from being attacked by Sarus's males at one of the settlements." He reached for a small oblong tool mounted on the wall behind the bench. "You all have a way about you that is hard to detect unless you are looking for it."

"I see." I turned, leaning sideways against the bench so I could observe his work without interfering. I had watched Cara perform similar tasks with Josh's tools for weeks, her skill and precision always amazing me. "As for Cara, I cannot discuss the reason for my presence, other than to assure you that I will not let any harm come to her."

Torrlun shook his head and snorted. "You do realize it is Cara who usually does the harming, do you not?"

"Yes, I am aware." I chuckled, then glanced into the adjoining room. Cara had taken a seat on one of the pillows scattered on the floor and was handing Rajak a block. Seeing her play with the young one reminded me of things I had learned not to yearn for long ago. Things I had given up when I became a warrior. With Khyron's new collaboration with Burke and the discovery of human female warriors, my life and my future held different possibilities.

"Does Cara know she is your ketiorra?" Torrlun's question surprised me, and I jerked my head, forcing my attention back to him.

"No." I rubbed my nape to ease the building tension. Even though I had done my best to disguise the fact, another ketaurran male could recognize the signs if they were paying attention. Apparently, Torrlun excelled at noticing details. "She is unlike most human females, even more independent than her friends."

"Which is why you have not shared your discovery with her yet." Torrlun extracted several small pieces off the part, then reached for another tool.

I nodded. Torrlun had grasped in minutes what had taken me days to determine.

"Would you like some advice?" he asked.

I was not arrogant enough to believe that when it came to Cara, I understood her motivations, nor would I turn down valuable insight from someone who had known her a lot longer. "If you think it would be helpful."

"You must, as the humans would say"—Torrlun laid down the tool and picked up the part to examine it more closely—"tread lightly."

I had heard the saying before but wasn't sure I truly comprehended its meaning. My expression must have relayed my confusion, because he grinned, then said, "Do not be overprotective. Unless you are willing to accept who she is, you will never earn her trust."

Protecting all females was part of a ketaurran male's nature. I had quickly learned from Laria, Celeste, and Sloane that it would not be tolerated, which gave me an advantage with Cara.

"Anything else?" I asked.

"You must let her realize she is your ketiorra on her own. Do not be eager with your affections; otherwise, she will never let you get close to her."

There was logic in his advice, yet I could not stop from being skeptical. "Are you certain what you have told me will work with Cara?"

"In many ways, Erin and Cara are a lot alike. So yes, I am quite certain." Torrlun glanced lovingly over his shoulder into the adjoining room, his wide smile fading. "It appears Cara is already demonstrating her need for independence and has elicited my ketiorra's help in the process."

I followed the direction of his gaze, noting that the pillow next to Erin was empty and Cara had disappeared from the room.

\*\*\*

*Cara*

Guilt was an emotion I'd learned to avoid, to push aside, to prevent from interfering on any of my missions. Yet, as I moved along the back streets of the village heading for the dwelling on the outskirts of the trader's market, the weight of how I'd deceived Zaedon pressed heavily against my chest. Running the justifications for my actions through my mind didn't help lessen the pressure.

There were a couple of males living close to Torrlun's home who I knew could provide me with the information on Doyle that I needed, but only one of them was reliable and could be trusted. Des, real name Desmond, was a bit eccentric and refused to do business with anyone who didn't address him by his nickname. I'd traded for information from him many times over the years and, so far, the data he'd given me had been accurate and he'd never betrayed my confidence.

The war had caused a lot of devastation, mostly to the human settlements, and many of the inhabitants living in Golyndier were wary of visitors, Des being at the top of the list. I'd been afraid he wouldn't be willing to trade if I'd brought Zaedon with me. Besides being ketaurran, he didn't exactly blend in well and could be intimidating to anyone who didn't know him. All it would take was one glance at his broad chest and firm muscles for Des to know there was a warrior hidden behind Zaedon's easygoing smile.

It was one of the reasons I used to convince myself that leaving Zaedon behind had been a good idea. That and the fact he wouldn't have agreed to let me go if I'd told him I was heading into the heart of the village where there were lots of people and the possibility of someone working for Doyle spotting me was a lot greater.

I moved along the outskirts of the crowded market, my head lowered so the hood of my jacket concealed most of my face.

The dull brown buildings in this area all had the same faded, run-down appearance. Multiple cracks covered the sandy mixture coating their exteriors. Des's place was no different, might even look worse. Overly cautious was the best way to describe the male who didn't like to draw attention to himself, and maybe he'd intentionally let the outside of his home slowly deteriorate.

After a couple of raps, I heard footsteps stop on the opposite side of the closed door. "Who's there?" Des barked, his deep, gravelly voice laced with apprehension.

I leaned forward, my mouth inches for the wooden surface. "Des, it's me, Cara."

Des whipped the door open, lips pressed firmly together and scowling. He stood a couple of inches taller than me, had light hair that was more brown than blond, and dark eyes that were currently narrowed. The male loved his weapons and had two blades strapped to his belt, one on each hip. I'd bet anything he also had a dagger hidden in at least one of his worn boots.

He grabbed my sleeve and pulled me inside, nervously glancing along the walkway in both directions, then slammed the door behind him. "You shouldn't be here." He enunciated each word, his tone chastising.

"Why?" I asked.

He'd been close to answering, then stopped himself with a groan. "You know the rules."

I nodded. "I do." The initial words spoken during each of our encounters might be a little different, but our conversation was always the same.

"Then you agree to the price." He didn't bother waiting for an answer before leading me to a room at the end of a short hallway. The room had no windows, and once inside, he activated the solars, giving the interior a soft glow.

After training with some of the males back at the settlement and learning to use my body as an effective fighting tool, I rarely carried any additional weapons, but over the years, I'd obtained quite a collection, most of them from Des. When the *Starward Bounty* was his home, he'd worked in operations and was an expert on a computer. Since ketaurran technology lacked the sophistication required to run a spaceship, he'd had to acquire another trade to survive. He'd taken to crafting blades of all lengths and sizes and had a large assortment of his work displayed on the long tables lining three of the room's walls.

"You've been busy." I walked over to the table on my left, running my fingertips along the hilts of several knives, admiring the ornate designs hand-carved into the handles. "These are very nice." I glanced over my shoulder to see his smile grow into a grin.

"This one." I pointed at a thin-bladed dagger. My friends were experts at wielding blades, especially Celeste, and were constantly teasing me about not keeping a knife attached to a sheath on my belt like they did. Sloane was the worst when it came to appreciating the weapons and was going to be jealous when I showed her the one with the blue-black blade I'd chosen to keep hidden in my boot.

"That one's five cradassons," Des said, tugging on his short beard.

"Fine." Telling him I thought the price was a little high would lead to haggling. If I'd had the time and wasn't worried about getting back to Torrlun's place, I would've talked him down to three.

Des held out his hand, patiently waiting from me to extract the coins from the pocket of my vest. Once our transaction was completed and I'd slipped the dagger into my boot, he asked, "What do you want to know?"

"What can you tell me about Doyle and the so-called price he has on my head?" As of two weeks ago, when

Vince had checked in with Zaedon, nothing had changed.

"From what I've heard, he wants you real bad." Des rubbed his chin, his dark eyes narrowing with concern. "Mind telling me what you did to get Doyle so riled?"

"Wish I could."

"You might also want to know that he's willing to pay an additional, and considerably larger, amount to get back whatever it was you stole."

When my friends and I rescued Vurell, a ketaurran physician, we'd taken the toxin the drezdarr had been poisoned with, along with its antidote. We'd arrived at Khyron's place in Aztrashar just in time to save his life.

During our escape, we'd also taken one of Doyle's solarveyors, which we later discovered had a hidden compartment containing a case of laser blasters. Following up on rumors and trying to discover if any of the weapons had survived the crash was the reason I'd infiltrated Doyle's compound in the first place.

At the end of the war, and after Sarus's reported death, his supporters had gone into hiding. If the laser weapons found their way into the hands of those supporters, they wouldn't hesitate to start another war, one that our side couldn't win with blades. If Doyle had offered a lot of money to get the weapons back, it wasn't hard to figure out whose side he supported.

I couldn't share any of the details, not without revealing the secret work I did for Burke. I was sure Des would have enjoyed hearing how I'd destroyed the labs in Doyle's compound so he couldn't reproduce any more of the toxin.

"Any idea who might be going after the reward seriously? Anyone local?" As far as I knew, there were only a handful of people who might be interested.

"No one who lives around here, at least not that I'm aware of," Des said.

"Thanks anyway." I turned to leave, and he placed a hand on my arm to stop me. "There's something else you might want to know."

"Yeah, and what's that?" I asked.

"There's been rumors, nothing I can substantiate yet, that Doyle's also involved with the group trying to kill the drezdarr. Some males met with a luzardee at the east-end bar not far from here a few weeks ago. As of a day or two ago, they were hanging around, so you might want to avoid going anywhere near that area of town. I would also suggest you hurry up with whatever business brought you here, and leave."

I knew the place he was talking about. I'd been there with Burke a couple of times. The meeting with the luzardee had happened right around the same time Khyron had been attacked at the settlement. His group already knew someone was trying to kill him, but none of them were aware that Doyle might somehow be involved. If it were true, it was something the vryndarr needed to know, starting with Zaedon.

It wasn't like Des to give out extra information, not without expecting some kind of payment. "Should I be picking out another blade?"

He shook his head. "That one's for free. Just make sure you let Burke know."

I shot him a questioning look, wondering how he knew about my relationship with Burke.

"Collecting information is my thing, remember?" He winked. "Now get out of here, and be careful who you trust."

# CHAPTER FOUR

*Zaedon*

"Erin, did Cara say where she was going?" My voice sounded strained as I struggled to remain patient and not take my irritation out on the female. It was not Erin's fault that Cara had chosen to leave without discussing her plans with me first. Not that I would have allowed her to leave, to risk putting herself in danger.

Had wherever she'd gone been a part of the reason she'd been adamant about making the trip to Golyndier? Knowing how devious she could be, it was not hard to assume leaving me behind had been her goal all along. And if the frustrating female had not already gotten herself killed, I was tempted to throttle her myself.

"I'm sorry, Zaedon, but no." Erin gripped Torrlun's arms, letting him do most of the work to get her off the floor. Once she was on her feet, she leaned back against Torrlun's chest, then gently rubbed her belly.

Rajak stepped in front of his dam, tipping his head backward to peer up at me. "Cara said it was a secret."

Though I admired Cara's ingenuity, I bit back a growl. She knew the child would reveal details if asked, and made sure not to give him any.

"Did she say anything else?" Torrlun asked.

Rajak turned his head to look up at his sire. "Only that we did not need to worry because she would not be gone long."

Not long when it came to Cara seemed like forever. I was raised from birth to be protective of all females. Learning to work with the human females, the ones adept at wielding blades and taking care of themselves, had been quite an adjustment. Even so, it did not prevent the overwhelming need to find my ketiorra and ensure her safety.

I glanced at Erin, who nodded her confirmation that what the young one had said was accurate.

"Zaedon." Rajak wrapped his small hand around one of my fingers and tugged.

"Yes." I looked down to see him staring up at me again, his nose wrinkled.

"Why do you think Cara stinks? Momma says it is not nice to say bad things about other people."

"What?" I remembered the comment I had made the first time Cara and I met. Had she assumed every time I sniffed her afterward that I was making a comparison? Had Erin told her the reason I constantly inhaled her scent was because she was my ketiorra?

If Cara had learned the truth from someone other than me, would it have prompted her to leave? I tried not to believe the worst, that Cara had put her life at risk because she wanted to get away from me.

I did not want to upset Rajak or his parents by voicing my concerns out loud. After running my hand along the side of my head, I knelt in front of the young one. "No, Rajak, I do not think she stinks. I think she smells wonderful."

Rajak crossed his little arms. "Good, because she is my friend, and I will not let anyone hurt her feelings."

Erin placed her hands on his shoulders. "Why don't

you go play with your blocks so we can talk to Zaedon?"

"Okay." He grinned, then walked across the room and plopped on the floor.

By the time I was back on my feet and following Torrlun and Erin into the adjoining room, the tightness gripping my chest had a firm hold on my stomach as well. "Does she know?" I asked Erin the second she stopped.

"She was curious, but I told her it was a discussion she needed to have with you."

"Then she did not leave because..." Some of the tension eased from my body.

"No, I think her reasons for not saying anything to you stemmed from something else." Erin gave me a sympathetic smile. "I'm pretty sure that not being able to tell you really bothered her... If that helps you any."

"It does, but not enough to keep me from going after her."

\*\*\*

Lately, rationalization when it came to Cara often eluded me. After hearing she was not aware that she was my ketiorra, at least not yet, and knowing she would not leave Golyndier without the repaired part for the harvester, it did not take me long to realize her reason for leaving might have to do with gaining information about her situation with Doyle.

Her motive was one I understood. Though it was information I did not readily share, Cara was not the only one whose capture came with a large reward. After Jardun's altercation with the luzardees in Aztrashar, then the attack on Khyron at the settlement not long after, we were aware that someone wanted the vryndarr and the drezdarr dead.

I had learned many admirable, sometimes frustrating things about Cara in the few weeks we had spent together. She cared greatly about the welfare of her family and the other humans. Even with a threat against her life, she was not the kind of female to stay in hiding long. After questioning Torrlun about possible places she might gain information, I followed his suggestion and made my first stop a bar located on the east end of town.

Utilizing my stealth training, a natural part of my daily existence, I kept my head covered and maneuvered through the streets of Golyndier. As with many other places I had visited, the war had left its devastating mark. Some areas, along with their inhabitants, took longer to recuperate than others. The humans I encountered on the walkways seemed wary of strangers and made sure to keep their distance.

The buildings in the outlying area lacked maintenance, the cracks in the exteriors more prominent than on those closer to the center of town. The bar's interior was not much better. The walls were bare, the overhead solars were not in use, making the late morning rays coming through a single pane the only light available.

A handful of humans occupied seats at several small wooden tables, drinking ale and conversing between themselves. The brief period of silence that greeted me the second I stepped into the room turned into the occasional stare and lowered muttering. Watching them from my periphery, I made my way to the long wooden counter situated in front of a wall shelved with darkened containers designed to hold liquids.

"What can I get ya?" the male behind the bar asked. He masked his wariness by reaching for an empty mug.

"I am looking for a female."

Disgust flared in his dark eyes. "We don't do that here. You'll need to go somewhere else."

I leaned closer, keeping my voice low. "I am not in need of a female to share my bed. I am searching for a specific female, one who would be seeking information."

"Sorry, can't help ya. I haven't had any females in here so far today." He set the mug back on the shelf. "You might have better luck at the market."

In my experience, information was rarely given freely without compensation. Since the male did not make the request and his nervousness seemed to stem from my presence, I had no reason to think he was hiding the truth. "Thank you for your time." After a nod from the male and one last glance at the others seated nearby, I left.

Torrlun had also mentioned he'd heard rumors of one or two others who provided information for a price. He could not give an exact location only that they could be found somewhere near the trader's market. Once I reached the busy area, I remained in the shadows of the surrounding buildings, avoiding attention and watching and listening to humans and ketaurrans barter over whatever they had to sell. I had yet to see any sign of Cara and was about to begin scouring the entire village when I spotted her leaving a nearby dwelling.

I was too far away to hear what she said to the human male standing in the doorway, but seeing her alive relieved some of my stress. The tension eased even more when she did not touch him in a way that suggested they had a strong familiarity with each other. It did not, however, alleviate the painful sting of her betrayal.

Cara adjusted the hood on her head, then glanced at her surroundings and headed in the opposite direction, away from the market. Curious to see if she would return to Torrlun's place or if she had another destination on her agenda, I kept my distance and followed her.

After passing several buildings, she turned onto the same narrow walkway we had used earlier. Instead of turning right as I'd expected, she turned left, disappearing from my sight.

Unwilling to lose her, I increased my stride, rounded the corner, and groaned when I found the passageway empty.

Wondering where the draeck she had gone, I didn't bother holding back a frustrated, near feral, growl.

Continuing forward was the only logical choice. I was halfway through the corridor when I heard the echo of footsteps coming from somewhere behind me.

An arm, moving rapidly, popped out from a narrow and darkened gap between the buildings, latching on to my sleeve and pulling me inside. Had I not caught Cara's unique scent, I might have reacted differently. Instead, I let her pin my back to the wall, her chest pressing firmly against mine.

"Someone is following you," she whispered in my ear, her warm breath caressing my skin and calming me further.

My tracking abilities were usually much better. If I hadn't been so distracted, Cara never would have detected my presence or gotten this close. Not that I minded having her body pressed against mine. I decided to take advantage of the situation by wrapping my arms around her waist. There was nothing I could do about my hardening shaft or the fact that she stopped squirming as soon as she had noticed.

The footsteps I had heard moved faster and got a lot closer, stopping shortly before reaching the gap where Cara and I were hiding.

"Where did he go?" a male asked loudly, seemingly unconcerned that he might be overheard, most likely by us.

"No idea," another male answered. "I could have sworn he came this way. After his chat with the bartender, I was sure he'd lead us to the female Doyle is looking for."

Cara tensed in my arms. I did not need to see her face to know she was glaring at me. In my anger and haste to find her, I had not considered there might be someone in the bar searching for her. If not for her quick actions, I would have led the males directly to her and possibly to the home of her friends.

"Maybe you're wrong and it's not the same female."

The first male spoke again. "I'll bet ten cradassons that

I'm right. Word has it she left the Quaddrien with some ketaurran males."

"Yeah, but if she left with the ketaurrans, then why would one of them be looking for her?"

"How should I know? All I'm saying is it's the best lead we've gotten so far. I'm getting tired of sitting around in the bar. What will it hurt to track the male and see if I'm right?"

There was a moment of silence before the second male answered. "Fine, let's circle around and see if he headed back toward the market."

Luckily, they did not pass our hiding spot, and I heard the sound of footsteps moving in the opposite direction.

Cara pushed against my chest until I released her. "Tell me you didn't go to the bar on the east end of town?"

"Cara, I…" I could not blame Torrlun for giving me the information, or for my decision to go there searching for her.

She placed a finger against my lips, the anger fading from her gaze. "We can talk about it later. Right now, I'd like to get back to Torrlun's place and see if he's done with the part."

The calmness in her voice was unsettling. For her to do nothing about those tracking her surprised me. "You do not wish to go after the males?"

"If getting back to the farm wasn't critical, I'd say yes." She leaned forward, peered in one direction, then the other before glancing back at me. "Besides, it didn't sound like they were going anywhere soon, so we can always come back later if we get bored and want to have some fun." With a wiggle of her brow, she took my hand and pulled me into the passageway.

# CHAPTER FIVE

*Cara*

By the time Zaedon and I made sure we weren't being followed again and had returned to Torrlun's home, my friend had completed repairing the part for the harvester. Erin had invited us to share their evening meal, and as much as I would've enjoyed spending more time with them, I knew it wouldn't be safe. For any of us.

If we'd had the time and the settlement wasn't farther away than my grandparents' place, I would've suggested we stop so I could relay the information Des had asked me to pass on to Burke.

The weather, in the form of a massive rain storm, had started shortly after Golyndier disappeared from the horizon, and was impeding our progress. After an hour of fighting conditions that continued to make driving difficult and letting Zaedon brood in silence—something totally out of character for him—I decided it was time to have our discussion.

"It's getting late, and the storm doesn't look like it's going to let up anytime soon." I chanced a glance in his direction to see if he was listening. I took his grunt as acknowledgment, then slowed the vehicle even more when it started to slide again.

"I think we should pull over and wait for the rain to stop." The base of the transport was set high off the ground, but maneuverability was horrible when the roads turned into muddy sand. Visibility was growing steadily worse, and with the uneven and worn areas on the road, I was concerned we'd either slide into a bordering rock wall or end up in one of the many nearby ravines.

The road wasn't heavily traveled, and the chance of anyone else being out here was slim. Most people hated being stranded and would have stopped, too afraid they might drain their solars. Based on our late-afternoon departure, I figured we had a few more hours of daylight left, not that it mattered with the storm blanketing the sky.

According to the controls, the transport's power registered at a decent level, enough to get us back to the farming community, if I was willing to push it.

Zaedon returned his gaze to the viewing pane, frowning at the surrounding darkness as if it was the first time he'd noticed it. "It would not be my first choice, but I would have to agree."

Glad to have his support, I stopped on a high spot in the middle of the road, leaving a comfortable distance between the transport and the ravine on our left.

I got out of my seat, took a much-needed stretch, then headed toward the back of the vehicle and opened one of the overhead storage units. "We still have some of Ellie's pyteinna left." I retrieved the container my grandmother had given me for the trip.

"Oooh, yes." I pulled out a storage cylinder filled with a clear brownish liquid and two of the mugs stacked on the shelf next to it. "Thank you, Laria." My friend might not be great about keeping supplies in the home she shared with Celeste and Sloane, and now Jardun, back at the settlement, but I could always count on her transport being stocked with some of Nayea's ale.

Nayea was an older ketaurran female who lived at the settlement and provided medical care to anyone who needed it. Besides mothering all of the males on Burke's team, she made the best ale I'd ever tasted.

After grabbing a couple of glow emitters and turning them on, I powered off the overhead solars to keep from draining the transport's engine.

Zaedon helped with the containers, then settled onto a bench seat across from me, the side of his long legs brushing against mine. After several bites and a few hefty swallows of Nayea's ale, Zaedon's mood seemed to lighten, the hint of a smile forming on his lips.

It seemed like a good time to start our talk. "Zaedon, I know you're upset, but before you say anything, I want you to know that what happened earlier wasn't your fault."

Zaedon's smile faded. "You mean when I put your life in danger by allowing the two males to follow me?"

I filled his mug to the top again, hoping it would help. "If anyone is to blame, it's me. I shouldn't have deceived you, and I'm sorry."

He took another long sip, studying me over the rim. "Why did you feel you could not tell me?" His voice was even, but I could tell by his tone that my actions had hurt him.

"You hadn't exactly been happy about making the trip. I was afraid if I told you why I wanted to leave, you'd try to stop me."

Zaedon held the mug on his lap and sighed. "I will admit I have been a little…"

"Overbearing, pushy, controlling," I added with a smile.

"I was going to say overprotective, but you have made your point." He grabbed another pyteinna. "Why did you go to see the human male?"

"I wanted more information about Doyle and what he's been doing." I'd spotted Zaedon shortly after talking to Des and assumed he'd seen me leaving his place. "My friend Des doesn't really trust ketaurrans."

"Another reason not to take me with you," Zaedon said.

"Yeah." I filled my mug for the third time, glad he understood my motivations, but hating how others viewed his people.

Even when Zaedon was doing his best to irritate me, I felt comfortable being around him. Besides being a good listener, he was also perceptive. "Is what and who I am a problem for you as well?"

"What? No." I coughed through my last swallow. "Why would you think such a thing?"

"Your opposition to my presence and insistence that I return to the settlement has been concerning."

No matter how hard I tried to fight it, I'd found myself caring about Zaedon, about what he thought and how he felt. I hadn't wanted to discuss Graham with anyone, ever. But Zaedon deserved better from me. He deserved to know the truth, to know the real reason I tried to keep him at a distance. "Neither of those things has anything to do with you, not personally, anyway."

I glanced at my lap, running fingertips along my mug, searching for the right words. I returned my gaze to his, the understanding in his turquoise eyes making it harder to tell him what I needed to say. "I had a partner once. Someone who worked with me. Someone I got involved with." I tipped my head back, draining the last of my ale, then said, "It ended badly." Getting out the words hadn't been as hard as I'd thought or as hurtful as I'd expected.

"How so?" He leaned forward and placed his hand on my leg.

"Something went wrong on one of our missions, and Graham was killed." I couldn't bring myself to give Zaedon any details and was glad that he didn't ask for any.

"It is why you work alone now, correct?"

It felt good to tell Zaedon about my past, but his uncanny perception could see the things I wanted to keep hidden, reminding me once again why it wasn't a good idea to let myself get close to him.

I wasn't prone to crying, but if I did more than nod, I'd end up sobbing and throwing myself into his strong, welcoming arms.

Pushing myself, along with the memories that needed to stay in the past, off the bench, I got to my feet. After several deep breaths, I opened another storage unit. "I don't know about you, but I could use some sleep. Celeste told me they sometimes spend the night in here when they travel." I heard him get up, could feel him standing behind me, and froze.

\*\*\*

*Zaedon*

I stood behind Cara, unsure what to say or do. Being assigned as her bodyguard without her permission had caused an unwanted tension between us, my overprotective actions earlier today only making things worse.

Her revelation about the male she had lost, a male whose bed she had most likely shared, gave me insight into her behavior and how to proceed with our relationship. We both had things in our past we would rather not talk about. It was our future, the one I hoped we would spend together, I was concerned about.

She was strong-willed, and if she had chosen to break down and shed tears for the memories of her past, I would have gladly taken her in my arms, comforted her with the caress of my tail. She was also a proud warrior, and if she chose to deal with her grief by remaining strong, then I would support her decision.

"Cara." When she didn't speak or move, I reached above her head and grabbed the blankets off the shelf. "I think getting some rest is a good idea."

The tense line in her shoulders disappeared, and she turned, giving me a thankful smile. "I hope you don't mind sleeping on the floor." She glanced from the benches, which were obviously too small to rest on comfortably, to the wide strip of metal flooring running from the control area to the back of the transport.

"It is better than some of the places I have slept." I handed her one of the blankets, then shook out the other before spreading it on the floor.

"The storm will make the evening temperatures drop much lower." I unhooked my belt and set it along with my sheathed blade off to the side, yet within reach in case we got unexpected visitors. The odds were low, but after being tracked by the males from the bar, I wasn't taking any more chances and wanted to be prepared.

I removed my jacket and rolled it to form a pillow, then sat along one side of the blanket. "We will stay much warmer if we sleep closer together." I patted the space next to me.

Cara wrinkled her nose. "Fine, but only if you promise to keep your hands"—she glanced behind me as an afterthought—"and your tail to yourself."

I chuckled, knowing what she asked was going to be extremely difficult. "I promise to do my best." I waited for her to settle in beside me and cover us with the other blanket before rolling on my side to face her.

Ketaurran metabolism was different from a human's. I hardly felt the effects of the potent ale. I was a little drowsy, but not quite ready to go to sleep.

We had yet to discuss her visit to see the male named Des, and though I was curious to hear what she had learned, I hoped bringing up the topic would not upset her again. "Did you learn anything of interest from the male you visited, anything you would like to share?"

"You mean other than confirming there's still a bounty on my head?" She rolled on her side, tucking the end of my jacket under her head and coating it with her scent.

"Yes, I did."

"Really?" I longed to nuzzle her neck and take a sniff, then remembered Cara's conversation with Erin and thought better of it. More than anything, I wanted Cara to trust me. Right now, what we shared was fragile, easily broken. The conversation we'd had was a step in making that happen. My earlier mistake with the males from the bar had not helped, but it was a mistake I did not plan on making again. When she did not answer right away, I decided not to push for the answer.

I'd gotten used to the skeptical way she studied me, as if she could see inside my mind and knew what I was thinking. "Don't you want to know what else I found out?"

"Only if you want to tell me."

"Uh-huh." Her grunt reminded me of the usual response my friend Garyck gave to most questions asked of him. The vryndarr was currently part of the group protecting the drezdarr and his ketiorra, Celeste, back at the settlement. "Des said he'd heard that not only did Doyle want what we took from the wastelands, he's also working with whoever is trying to kill Khyron. The males who are searching for me also met with some luzardees at the east end bar. I'm guessing it was the same luzardees who attacked our friends."

She did not use a chastising tone when she mentioned the bar, yet it did not stop me from cringing. If Doyle was truly involved with those plotting to harm Khyron, how many more mercs were active participants? It was troubling news and something my friend needed to be made aware of. Delaying the news for a few more days would not change Khyron's plans to unite the humans and the ketaurrans. "Perhaps as soon as the harvest is over, we should take a trip to the settlement so you can tell Khyron and Burke what you have learned yourself."

Cara narrowed her eyes and poked my chest. "How much ale did you drink?"

"Why would you ask me such a question? You are the one who filled my glass and already know the answer."

She giggled. "It's a human thing based on curiosity. Yesterday, you were dead set against me leaving my grandparents' place, and now"—she flicked her wrist—"you're okay with traveling around the countryside."

"I see." I smiled and brushed some loose curls off her cheek.

She didn't try to push me away, only narrowed a mischievous cinnamon gaze at my hand. "You're touching me."

"I said I would try not to, but if we are being honest, you touched me first." I let my hand drop over hers and kept it there.

"Fair enough, but that still doesn't explain why you're okay with me returning to the settlement."

Admitting I had erred to myself was a lot easier than stating the fact out loud, yet with Cara, it came easily. "Had I not been acting in an overprotective manner, you would not have been compelled to leave on your own and seek information without me."

"You're probably right." She yawned and closed her eyes.

"Might I suggest a truce of sorts?"

Her eyelids fluttered drowsily, and the way she snuggled against my jacket made me wish it was my shoulder.

"Cara," I said when she didn't respond.

"Yeah, sounds good."

When her eyes did not open again, I turned off the glow emitters, then scooted closer to her. Breathing in her scent did not help the hardened state of my shaft, but having her near allowed the rest of my body to relax and slowly follow her toward sleep.

# CHAPTER SIX

*Cara*

Wondering what had startled me from my deep slumber, I forced one eye, then the other, open. Sunlight streamed through the transport's viewing panes, signaling the early morning and an end to the storm. My back was pressed against Zaedon's chest, his arm draped across my waist, the end of his tail encircling my ankle. Heat from his body surrounded me, and for the first time in a long time, I felt safe and protected.

My brain was a little fuzzy about the previous night's events. I remembered telling him to keep his hands to himself. When my thoughts cleared, I realized Zaedon had kept his word—well, sort of. I still had my clothes on, and nothing had happened other than drinking too much of Nayea's ale and falling asleep together. I could rationalize all the reasons getting close to Zaedon was a bad idea as much as I wanted. It wouldn't change the fact that I cared about him and yearned to run my hands over his scales as I stripped him naked.

The heavy footsteps I heard crunching on the sand outside the solarveyor must have been what had wakened me. We were too far from any inhabitable places, which meant another vehicle had arrived while we were sleeping.

"Darn it, I can't see inside. The panes are too high." I heard a female's slightly muffled voice, followed by an irritated smack against the hull's exterior. "Do you think it's abandoned?"

"Must be. Otherwise, whoever owned it would be out here already," a male voice answered. "Let me get my tools and see if I can bypass the security on the access door." The male's voice faded along with his footsteps.

"Zaedon," I whispered, then wiggled, trying to dislodge myself.

He nuzzled the side of my neck. "Be still, my vrincorra. It is early yet."

Hadn't he heard the conversation going on outside? And why had he called me the name of a rare flower in his native tongue? The vibrant jade blossoms were beautiful, similar to an Earth rose, but impossible to pick because of all the thorny leaves surrounding them. I couldn't tell if he was sleeping, dreaming, or trying to be cute. When his arm tightened around my waist instead of letting me go, I elbowed him in the ribs.

With a groan, he grabbed his side, his eyes popping open. "Cara, what the draeck?"

I rolled away from him. "Snuggle time is over, handsome."

"Handsome. Does that mean you find me appealing?" Only Zaedon could make swishing his tail look so adorable.

"Yes, I... You are unbelievable." I got on my hands and knees, then crawled toward the access door. "Now get over here. We have guests."

His grin faded. "Is it the males from the village?" He pushed off the floor into a crouching position.

"No, it's a male and a female, possibly scavengers or road bandits." I glanced at him over my shoulder. "From what I could hear, they seemed more interested in the transport than anything else."

He grinned and moved to join me, grabbing his knife off the floor on his way. "Good, then they will be easy to dispense with." He retrieved his blade, then set the sheath off to the side with his belt.

It wasn't long before our unwanted visitors returned and the male went to work on the exterior lock. I wasn't in the mood to make more repairs and decided to open the door before he could do any damage. "Ready?" I whispered to Zaedon, getting a nod before releasing the access.

We never got to execute our attack. A tall human male with dirt smudging his face, wearing worn clothes that appeared and smelled as if they hadn't been cleaned in over a week, leaned through the entryway. "Surprise!" He jabbed a stun stick into Zaedon's ribs.

Ketaurran males were strong, could withstand a lot of pain, yet a single jab from the stick had Zaedon snarling and his body jerking. The blade dropped from his hand, clanking against the metal floor seconds before he fell backward next to me with his eyes closed.

"Zaedon!" I yelled, then noticed the female had a stick of her own and was thrusting it in my direction. I scooted backward to avoid being shocked, the metal tip barely missing my leg.

The male admired his handiwork. "That luzardee wasn't kidding when he said these were strong enough to knock out a ketaurran." The male eyed Zaedon, then me. "Best trade I ever made. Maybe he'll be willing to trade another one for you and the lizard."

"What I can't believe is how easy they made it for us." The female playfully smacked the male's arm, then sneered at me. Her clothes weren't much better, but her face was a little cleaner, the bridge of her nose and cheeks covered with freckles. "Did you really think we'd be stupid enough to open the door without being armed first?"

I almost said *yes*, but figured it would earn me a poke

with the stick and thought better of it.

The male sneered at me, then snickered. "Nobody just up and leaves a transport out here unattended. We knew you had to be inside. That's why we were practically yellin' what we planned to do."

I glared at the bandits, calculating the odds of disarming one before the other had a chance to stun me.

The male must have guessed what I was thinking. He held the tip of his stick near Zaedon's chest. "It's also powerful enough to kill, so unless you want to say goodbye to your friend permanently, I suggest you cooperate."

I hadn't realized how much I cared about Zaedon until the thought of witnessing his death slammed into my chest. Unwilling to risk finding out whether or not the male was bluffing, I held up my hands and sat back on my haunches.

"That's a good girl." He kept his focus on me and spoke to the female standing next to him. "Bev, go get the shackles."

"You got it," she said with a grin.

While his partner was off doing his bidding, I continued to glare, mentally planning the numerous ways I was going to exact revenge for the pain he'd caused Zaedon.

\*\*\*

*Zaedon*

With a groan, I struggled to open my eyes, grasping for reasons why I could not move my arms. I wondered why the aching throb pulsing along my forehead was a close match to the pain radiating along my ribs, then remembered the human male who had jabbed me with a stun stick.

Ketaurrans could tolerate a lot of pain, the vryndarr conditioned to bear even more. I had been stunned with a stick before, the shock never anything more than an annoyance. This was the first time the current had forced me into unconsciousness. It was obvious the stick had been modified, the voltage increased, turning it into a weapon with lethal capabilities.

Once the hazy condition of my brain began to clear, worried thoughts of Cara filled my mind. Had she endured the same torturous treatment? Was she still alive?

"Zaedon, if you can hear me, don't move or draw attention to yourself." Cara's whispered warning came with a nudge to my shoulder.

Hearing her voice went a long way toward helping me relax. I immediately stilled, keeping my eyes narrowed so I could take in our surroundings. I was seated on the ground, my wrists and ankles shackled, my back braced against a tree, which, luckily, only grew sharp thorns along the upper branches and not along the trunk.

Judging by the diminished sunlight filtering through the upper branches, hours had passed and evening was approaching. We were situated in a large clearing, the sandy surface flat with signs of wear, the only apparent way in or out a single road off to the left.

Besides our transport, there were two others parked on the opposite side of the clearing, and beyond them was the beginning of several rock formations. Mumbled voices echoed through the air, and I caught glimpses of two human males moving between the vehicles, the female I had seen early nowhere in sight.

Without turning my head, all I could see of Cara were her wrists, bound with similar shackles, and her legs extended on the ground in front of her. The humans had not bothered to bind her feet. It was an oversight they would not have made if they had been aware of her fighting abilities. "Are you unharmed?"

"I'm fine, but what about you? You took one heck of a hit." The concern in her voice was more soothing than any healing salve.

"I will survive." It would take another day before the pain was no longer noticeable.

"Good, because if you ever scare me like that again, I'll hurt you myself."

"It was not as if I could have foreseen what would happen." I turned my head slowly so I could see her face. "You were worried about me?"

She shrugged. "No, I didn't want to explain to Khyron how my bodyguard ended up in worse shape than when I got him."

I concealed my laughter with a snort, knowing that Khyron would not care. He had seen me with far worse injuries.

Cara kept her gaze focused on the humans, who, so far, had not paid any attention to us. "We need to find a way out of here before they figure out who we are and decide to turn us in for the bounty."

"Us?" Whoever had wanted Khyron dead had also set a price for all the vryndarr, myself included. I wanted to know who had given my friend the deadly toxin, the treacherous piece of chaugwas dung whose life I intended to end should I ever discover their identity.

At the moment, it wasn't nearly as important to me as getting Cara to safety. Over the past few weeks, I had grown to care for her deeply. She was my ketiorra, and, if something happened to her, there would never be another female for me.

"Des might have mentioned that the vryndarr are worth a few cradassons. I guess you forgot to tell me, or it must have slipped your mind, since you were too busy being overprotective."

"It did not seem relevant to keeping you safe."

"Relevant or not, in the future, I'd appreciate a heads-up." She punctuated her frown with a stern glare.

Her use of the word future held the promise of possibilities and warmed me to my core. I thought it best not to question her further and concentrated on a way out of our current situation.

"How many are in their group?" I asked.

"I counted five—the two who attacked us and three others who arrived in the other solarveyor." Cara slowly adjusted the way she was sitting by pulling her legs closer to her body.

"What are you doing?" I asked.

"Getting us out of here, remember?" She smiled and worked a thin-bladed dagger out of her boot.

The female was always surprising me. As far as I knew, she preferred to use her fists, had no use for weapons. This was the first time since we had left the settlement that I actually saw her handle a blade.

She noticed the direction of my gaze and spoke before I could ask. "I got it from Des. Buying one of his handcrafted weapons is the price for information." If he was one of her sources, then I had no doubt she possessed an extensive collection, one I planned to have her show me later.

"Mind keeping an eye on our friends and letting me know if anyone looks in our direction?" she asked, then went to work on the lock.

I watched the humans as she asked, stealing an occasional glimpse at her effort. After several minutes, I heard a click, and the metal cuffs loosened on her wrists. "Done." She placed the blade on the ground next to my leg and pushed against the trunk until she was standing. "I hope you know how to pick a lock."

"Cara, what happened to our truce and sharing information?" I growled through gritted teeth, my breath wasted because she had already disappeared into the surrounding darkness.

Was she getting even because she had learned about the threat to the vryndarr from Des and not me? I swallowed a frustrated groan and reached for the dagger. Two of the other humans Cara mentioned moved into my view, and I froze, not wanting to draw their attention.

While the one who was tall, lanky, and had a tousled head of reddish-brown hair set up portable glow emitters, the other, a shorter and wider version of the first, prepared a fire for cooking.

It would not be long before they noticed Cara was missing. If we got out of here alive, Cara and I were going to have a discussion about sharing details of her plans before executing them.

I had barely removed the cuffs around my wrists when Cara slowly appeared from behind one of the transports, her fingers wrapped around what appeared to be a large rock. What was the female thinking? I hurried to open the other lock, my attention divided between whatever crazy thing Cara was about to do and freeing my ankles.

"Hey, asshole!" Cara shouted.

I grinned, admiring her choice of human curse words and the fact that it had been directed at the male who had stunned me.

Even more admirable was her throw. It caught the male on the side of the head, eliciting a yelp and causing him to stagger a few steps backward.

The other four members of the human group were on their feet and two of them were reaching for the stun sticks. Cara did not stay to fight as I'd expected. Instead, she raced back the way she came, once again disappearing from my sight.

The female joined the others, her arms wrapped around two containers, one stacked on top of the other. "Lloyd, what happened?" she asked as soon as she saw the male holding the side of his head, dropping the containers in her haste to get to him.

"The female got loose." The male winced when she pulled his hand away to examine his injury.

"What?" There's no way she should have been able to get out of those shackles." The female's tone was filled with disbelief.

"Well, she did."

The female pointed in my direction. "Look, the ketaurran's getting away too."

The tall, thin male held a stun stick out to his wider look-alike. "You go after the female and bring her back. I'll take care of the ketaurran."

"No." The male who'd been injured with the rock pushed to his feet. "I owe the female for what she did to my head. I'll go." He grabbed a stick out of the other male's hand.

Normally, I had no problem entering a fight when the odds were not in my favor. Injuries I could handle, but a jab from one of those sticks would incapacitate me again, leaving Cara to battle alone. It was a risk I was not willing to take. I grabbed the shackles off the ground, hoping to put them to use, then followed her lead and headed into the thickly wooded area behind me.

# CHAPTER SEVEN

*Cara*

Now that the storm had passed, the remaining sunlight provided enough illumination for me to see where I was going. After throwing the rock at the male who'd hurt Zaedon—an extremely satisfying experience—I circled around the clearing to the spot where we'd been shackled. It wouldn't do Zaedon and me any good to get Trixie and leave. The bandits would just follow us, and I was more afraid of what Laria would do to me if her transport got damaged again.

The only way to make sure that didn't happen was to incapacitate them and drain the solars in their vehicles, which wouldn't leave them permanently stranded. It would take them at least a day to recharge, provided they had full sunlight, and give us plenty of time to make it back to the farming community without being followed.

I also wanted to get my hands on those stun sticks. First to keep our attackers from using them on anyone else and, second, to get a closer look at them and see how they'd been modified. Maybe it was something Josh could reproduce once his fingers were healed.

If that was possible, I knew for certain Burke and his guys would love to add them to their weapons collection.

Zaedon and the shackles were gone, but before I could figure out where he went, a firm, broad chest pressed up against my back, a hand clamping over my mouth.

"Cara, it is me," Zaedon whispered in my ear, then dropped his hand but didn't move the arm encircling my waist.

The vryndarr were trained to move with stealth when necessary, which was why I hadn't heard his approach. Even if he hadn't said anything, after waking in his arms this morning, I would have known it was him. "I kind of figured." I smiled, enjoying the protective way his tail was wrapped around my ankles.

"Can I assume you had a plan when you attacked the male with a rock?" I heard the humor in Zaedon's voice but was distracted by his lips, which were inches from my neck, his warm breath causing shivers along my skin.

It was hard to concentrate with him this close, so I tapped his arm, urging him to release me. "A distraction to give you time to get free. And maybe to get a little revenge for you." I shrugged. No point in lying.

"Beautiful and devious." He reached for my hips and pulled me closer.

"Zaedon, we…" Telling him we didn't have time for this seemed unimportant after his mouth covered mine in a possessive kiss that lasted only seconds.

Once he released me and I could think clearly again, I said, "The males with the stun sticks are already moving away from the other three in the group. If we take out the unarmed ones first, we shouldn't have a problem going after the other two together."

Our discussion was interrupted by rustling in the underbrush to our right, followed by a male voice. "Lloyd, any sign of them?"

"Not yet, but they couldn't have gone far," the other male said. "No one can survive out here for very long. My guess is they'll go for their transport, which is why I have Jeff and Evan watching it. There's no way they'll let the female and the lizard get inside."

"Good, then let's split up, cover more ground."

Zaedon reached for the shackles lying on the ground next to his feet, then motioned for me to lead in the opposite direction. If Lloyd's insult had bothered Zaedon, he'd masked his reaction well. Personally, hearing it disgusted me, and I muttered, "Sounds like I need to find another rock."

***

*Zaedon*

Cara's warrior spirit constantly amazed me. It was hard not to proudly puff out my chest after hearing she had purposely injured the male who had stunned me as retribution for the pain he had caused, then threatened to go after Jeff as well for calling me a lizard.

It was not the first time I had been insulted, and I was certain it would not be the last. Some humans had not adjusted well to being stranded on a strange planet with no hope of returning home, and it showed in the way they treated my people.

I did not care what the bandits thought of me. All that mattered was how Cara viewed me. Observing her protective nature reinforced my hope that when I finally told her she was my ketiorra, I would be able to convince her we were meant to be together.

Cara glanced over her shoulder. "What do you say we start with the two guarding the transport?" She was already heading in that direction, moving in a wide enough circle so we did not cross paths with the two males wielding sticks.

When we reached the trees near the vehicles, she stopped and peered around a thick trunk. "They're armed with blades, so we're going to need a distraction." She playfully rolled her gaze over me from top to bottom. "I might think you're kind of cute, but I don't think the two males guarding the access door will be interested in you."

"A chonderra is cute." I huffed. "I am a warrior and would rather be compared to one of your Earth lizards than have my appearance compared to a furry creature young ones consider a pet."

"If you already know you're good-looking, then you don't need me to tell you." The shake of her head included a roll of her dark eyes. "Besides, Fuzzball is very good at snuggling."

Fuzzball was the chonderra that belonged to the human young ones living with Harper back in the settlement. I could not resist the opportunity to defend myself with a little teasing. "You did not seem to mind my snuggling capabilities last night. As a matter of fact…"

She cut me off. "I… You… Now is not the time to have this discussion." She turned her attention back to the two males. "Why don't I do the distracting and you can sneak up on them from behind?"

"What about their weapons? If the males have experience with blades, it might take longer to disarm them." I did not mention my concern that she could be harmed in the process.

"If you need my help, just say so." She tugged on the front of her shirt, exposing more of her ample breasts and making it difficult to stop staring or keep my shaft from hardening.

I scowled, not happy that other males would see what I so desperately wished to touch.

She followed the direction of my gaze and grinned. "Yeah. Not going to be a problem at all."

"If you are done teasing, shall we?" I snarled at the treacherous female who was going to be my undoing.

With a giggle, she slipped past the rear of the vehicle, stepping into view of the other males. "Hey, guys. I don't suppose you'd be willing to let me take my transport and leave if I were to give you something in return, would you?" Cara approached the males with an enticing swagger.

As she'd predicted, both males stared at her chest. One even licked his lips. Voices carried in the clearing. I could hear their conversation as I quickly slipped around the transport.

"Depends on what you had in mind," one of the males said.

The males had shifted their positions and had their backs to me by the time I reached the opposite end of the vehicle.

"Wait, Jeff, it could be a trap." The male placed a warning hand on his friend's arm. "What about the ketaurran? You know how protective they are of females. I don't think he would have left her alone."

"Well, that's where you're wrong," Cara said. "He was afraid you'd shock him again and took off. So I'm all alone."

I had never seen Cara pout, but she managed it quite nicely, making me wonder how often she had used similar performances.

"Sooo, who wants to go first?" Cara inched a little closer to the males, keeping their attention on her and away from me.

"I'll go," Jeff said as he returned his blade to the sheath on his belt and walked over to the transport's access door. He turned to the other male. "You can stay out here and keep watch."

"What about the others? What do I tell Lloyd if he shows up and asks where you are?"

Jeff swiped his hand through his hair, pausing briefly on his nape. "Damn, Evan, you worry too much. By the time he realizes the ketaurran is long gone and gets back, I'll be done. Then you can have your turn."

Cara walked up to Jeff and slipped her hands across his shoulders. "You should have listened to your friend." A well-placed hit with her knee had the male doubling over and grabbing his groin. If not for the circumstances, I might have empathized with his moan of excruciating pain.

"You little bitch." Evan lunged for Cara, but before he could get near her, I grabbed his arm, careful to keep the blade away from my body, then spun him around and slammed him headfirst into the vehicle. With a loud thump and a groan, he dropped to ground next to his friend.

Satisfied he would not be getting back up anytime soon, I glanced in Cara's direction. She was flexing the fingers on her right hand and hovering over Jeff, who was also lying on the ground unconscious. "Two down, three to go."

"I heard voices." The female from the group picked that moment to come sauntering into view. "Any sign of them yet?" With a gasp, she skidded to a stop, then glanced from the two downed males to Cara and me.

It took only a second for her to realize what had happened, then back up a few steps and turn to run. "Lloyd!" she screeched. "They're over…"

Cara was closer and reacted quickly. She launched herself at the female, locking an arm tightly around her neck and bringing her to her knees. The female made a muffled squeak. Her clawing and flailing attempts to remove Cara's arm were futile. Within seconds, the loss of air hastened her trip into darkness. "Make that two to go," Cara said as she released her hold and carefully lowered the female to the ground.

"That was most impressive." I held out my hand and helped Cara to her feet.

She grinned. "Just something I picked up from Logan."

I had learned from Celeste that all her female friends had received a great deal of training from Burke's second-in-command. It was my understanding he did not hold back during their workouts and could be quite vicious.

Cara knelt on the ground next to Jeff, unhooking his sheath and blade.

I did the same with Evan, tucking the weapon into the back of my pants.

She tucked the knife into her boot and said, "We should get the shackles for these three before we go look for the others."

"Bev!" Lloyd's concerned voice boomed from the other side of the vehicle. "Where are you?"

"Looks like the shackles will have to wait." She patted my cheek. "Do me a favor and don't get zapped again." Then she was off, circling around the closest solarveyor and moving toward the other males.

"Cara," I growled through gritted teeth, swishing my tail and chasing after her. If I could shed scales, her continual need to rush into danger would surely cost me many.

I moved to the edge of the clearing. The glow emitters were activated, lighting the surrounding area and casting shadows. The males stood several feet apart and were glaring into the wooded area beyond the nearest transport.

"Where'd she go?" the male whose name I had yet to learn asked Lloyd.

Cara must have shown herself long enough to get their attention, then disappeared again. A smart tactic if her goal was to separate them.

"It is not the female you should be concerned with." I walked into the clearing, making sure to keep plenty of distance between me and the two males.

"Go after her." Lloyd motioned to the other male with a tip of his head.

Lloyd waited for the other male to comply, then said, "So, you decided to come back for more, did ya?" He tightened his grip on the stick, warily easing toward me.

"It is not me who will be feeling the effects of your weapon," I said.

Uncertainty flashed in Lloyd's dark eyes. His faltering led to a glance around the abandoned clearing before he shouted, "Jeff, Evan, get your asses over here."

I tried not to think about the other male going after Cara, the possibility of something going wrong and her getting hurt. Instead, I concentrated on Lloyd. I mimicked his steps, flexing my fingers and looking forward to our upcoming battle. "Your friends will not be able to help you."

Lloyd's glare turned feral. "What about Bev? If she's hurt, I'll do more than stun you."

"The female is unharmed, only sleeping with the others."

Lloyd growled and lunged at me, the shocking end of the stick aimed at my chest.

I had been ready for his attack, calculating the seconds before impact. Anger led to mistakes, and Lloyd realized his too late when I sidestepped, then grabbed the same end of the stick he held. Strength was my advantage, and I used it to twist the weapon until the point touched his midsection.

He groaned, his body spasming, his grip on the stick loosening. His death was not my intention, so as soon as he dropped to his knees, I yanked the stick out of his hands and away from his body. The dose he received was strong, and he crumpled to the ground unconscious.

Cara was an excellent fighter, but it did not prevent me from being concerned for her safety. While I had been busy with Lloyd, she had lured the other male back into the clearing. I turned to find her easily dodging the other male's attempt to stun her.

"Do you require assistance?" I asked, but did not move to help her.

"Nope, I've got this." She spun to the right, the next swipe barely missing her chest.

The male must have been worried I would interfere anyway and made the mistake of glancing in my direction. It was the opening Cara needed to avoid being shocked and land a hard blow to the male's midsection with her foot.

With an expulsion of air, he lost his balance and staggered backward. The stick went flying, clanking off the transport's metal exterior. Cara finished what she started with another kick, this one more centered, the force sending the male to the ground. Temporarily winded, the male grabbed his chest and gasped for air. "You b…" He rolled on his side, attempting to get up.

I did not give him the chance to finish insulting Cara and used the stick I had taken from Lloyd to jab him in the leg, sending him into a deep sleep like the others.

Cara moved next to me, brushing my shoulder with hers. "And you thought *I* had a vicious side."

"I thought it only fair the male know what others felt when he used his weapon on them," I said.

"Lucky for us they didn't think I was much of a threat and hadn't bothered to knock me out after they zapped you."

"A mistake I am sure they will regret once they awaken." I chuckled.

"Probably so." She smugly smiled at the unconscious males. "Anyway, I got a good look out of the viewing pane, and I'm pretty sure I know where we are." Cara knelt beside the closest solarveyor, then rolled on her back and scooted underneath.

"What are you doing?"

"Making sure they can't follow us." She reappeared, taking my offered hand to get back on her feet. "Unless one of them is a good mechanic, it will take them some time to figure out that I disconnected the solars." She walked over to their other vehicle and did the same thing.

"Now we can go." She grabbed the other stick off the ground on her way to Laria's transport. "This might come in handy. I'll have Josh take a look at it. Maybe he can make some more for Burke and the guys. Who knows, maybe I might need to keep one for myself." She winked. "They seem to work well on overbearing ketaurrans."

I gave her teasing comment the snort it deserved and

clutched the stick I held to my chest rather than give it to her.

She quirked a brow. "Worried?"

"You can be rather intimidating." Her laughter and the enticing view I got of her backside as I followed her to our transport made my tail tingle.

# CHAPTER EIGHT

*Cara*

I was glad I'd had the foresight to stick the bag containing the repaired part in one of the transport's upper storage units. When Bev searched Trixie looking for anything of value after she'd shackled Zaedon and me, she'd assumed the part was a spare and had ignored it.

With decent weather and the drive to my grandparents' home about an hour away from the clearing where we'd left the bandits, we'd arrived after they'd retired for the night. If Ellie and Isaac followed their usual preharvesting routine, they'd gone to bed early.

It had been a good thing, because after the adventurous day I'd had, I wasn't in the mood for answering questions. And Ellie was notorious for conjuring up a few. Not that I'd avoided her questioning altogether. She had plenty of them ready to go by the time I returned to the house after getting up early to install the repaired part in the harvester. The installation had gone quicker than I'd expected, giving me time to start cooking breakfast before Ellie joined me and took over.

I sat at the table in the kitchen, sipping a fresh cup of

freegea. "Did your visit with Erin and Torrlun go well?" my grandmother asked.

My friends had stayed here the few times they'd visited the community. "They're doing great. Rajak has grown quite a bit, and Erin looks like she's going to pop any minute."

"I've heard ketaurrans can tell the sex of their children before they're born." Ellie crossed her arms and bobbed her head as if the information she'd shared was more of a fact than a rumor.

"Really? I'd never heard that before," I scoffed.

Ellie crinkled her nose. "What did Torrlun have to say about it?"

"He's convinced the baby is a female." I took another sip.

"There you have it, then."

"There you have what?" Zaedon strolled into the kitchen, his shoulder-length hair damp from a recent shower, his glistening blue scales begging to be touched.

Warmth spread throughout my body, and I raised my cup to my lips to hide any possible drooling.

"Let me." Ellie took the mug he'd been reaching for and filled it with freegea before setting it on the table and encouraging Zaedon to take the empty seat next to me.

"Thank you." Zaedon sat in the chair, scooting it just enough to invade my personal space. He lifted the cup to his lips, then eyed me expectantly over the rim, waiting for me to answer his question.

Once the flutter in my stomach from being this close to him calmed, I glanced at my grandmother, expecting her to say something, and got nothing more than a shrug. With a sigh, I finally said, "Ellie's convinced ketaurran males can predict the sex of a child before it's born."

"She is correct." Zaedon shared a grin with Ellie.

"Seriously?" Besides being curious, it irritated me that the two of them always seemed like they were conspiring against me. "Could you tell the baby was going to be a female too?"

Zaedon's cheeks flushed, and he shifted uncomfortably in his seat as if he needed to carefully select his words before answering. "No, only Torrlun could tell, because Erin is his ketiorra."

"I see." I wasn't sure why he continued to squirm, but I found myself enjoying it. "So if…"

"Did you know Cara already fixed the harvester?" Ellie interrupted, then set a plate of pyteinnas in front of Zaedon.

"Why did you not wake me to help?" I hated hearing the hint of rejection in his voice.

"Today's going to be a long day. I thought you might like to sleep in, maybe get a little extra rest." I remembered my restless night of sleep, my thoughts continually drifting to Zaedon. The stun from the stick had caused him more pain than he admitted. He'd tried to hide it, but I'd seen him wince a couple of times when he disarmed Lloyd.

I quickly glanced at his ribs, then held his gaze, hoping he'd know I was referring to his injured side without asking me to give any details in front of Ellie. I had no intention of telling her about our adventure with the bandits and needed Zaedon's silence on the subject to keep it that way.

Zaedon's injury wasn't the only reason I had for wanting to get up early and work on the harvester alone. The other had to do with what Des told me about someone paying to get rid of the vryndarr. I couldn't stop wondering if Zaedon, I, or both of us had been targeted by whoever had sabotaged the part for the harvester.

I didn't want to take a chance that something else had been done while we were gone. After I'd installed the part, I did a thorough examination of the engine and was relieved that nothing else had been tampered with.

"I didn't expect you to help with the harvest, so it's okay if you want to hang out here with Ellie." After yesterday, things had changed between us, into what I wasn't sure, but I'd actually looked forward to spending the day with him and was going to be disappointed if he decided to stay behind.

"After all the preparations I have assisted with, I would not miss it." He flashed me a beaming smile, reached for a flat cake, then devoured it in seconds.

"Okay, then." I downed the last of my freegea, then walked over to the counter and began filling a container with the remaining pyteinnas.

A few seconds later, Zaedon moved in behind me and snatched a pyteinna out of the container before I closed it. After taking a bite, he made a happy rumbling noise. "Ellie, these are very good, possibly the best you have made since I arrived."

"It's not me you should be complimenting." Ellie grinned, the wrinkles around her eyes deepening. "Cara made them."

Zaedon coughed, nearly spitting out the cake. "You know how to prepare food?"

"I have many talents." I crossed my arms and glared. "One of which is being able to kick your butt if you don't stop looking so surprised."

"There will be no kicking of anyone's backside in the house." Ellie picked up the container and shoved it into Zaedon's arms. "Now go. No doubt Isaac is already waiting for you two."

Zaedon grabbed two more of the flat cakes off a plate on our way out of the kitchen, quickly eating them before we reached the door. I didn't think I'd ever get over how much the male consumed. Maybe it was the reason he had such a ripped body, not that I was going to ask.

I grabbed a large bag I'd filled with water cylinders earlier, strapping it over my shoulder on my way out the door. Once we were outside and had cleared the platform, I held out my hand. "I'll take that."

He groaned, his frown the adorable kind I'd seen Rajak make. After he reluctantly released the container, I stuffed it inside my bag. "You can have as many as you want later when we stop for lunch."

We were halfway to the area where the harvester was parked when Ellie called Zaedon's name. We both stopped and turned to see my grandmother standing in the doorway, holding up another container. "In case you need a snack," she said.

Zaedon grinned, swished his tail, and called, "I will catch up" over his shoulder as he hurried back to the house.

I shook my head and continued walking without him. When I rounded the corner of the building, I found Derrick sitting next to my grandfather on the bench mounted to the floor in front of the harvester's control panel.

"Morning, Cara." Derrick was the first to acknowledge my arrival with a once-over glance at my entire body. I covered my nausea and disappointment with a fake smile. I could tolerate Derrick, easily ignore him if he bothered me, but his dislike of Zaedon grated along every one of my nerves. Putting them together for more than a few minutes was asking for trouble.

"Morning." I aimed the greeting at my grandfather.

"Morning, sweetheart. How's my little girl?" It didn't matter how old I got, Isaac always addressed me the same as he had when I was a child.

Other than the silver sprinkling the dark hair along his temples and a few wrinkles around his mouth and eyes, Isaac was fit and could pass for a male ten years younger.

"Your little girl is fine, thanks." I reached for the bars mounted on each side of the opening and hoisted myself inside. "Where's Josh? I thought he was riding with us today."

The interior design of the partially enclosed space wasn't anything fancy, mostly constructed to protect the control unit and anyone sitting inside from the weather. It resembled a large metal box sitting on a platform above the harvester unit. It was open on both sides and had a viewing pane running along the front above the controls.

Derrick scooted closer to Isaac, making room on the bench for me to sit next to him.

"That's okay, I'll sit back here." I slid across the additional bench until I was sitting behind my grandfather.

Isaac shifted sideways to face me. "Zaedon coming?"

"He's on his way." I slipped the strap to my bag off my shoulder, placing it on the floor between my feet. "Apparently, Ellie is under the impression he might starve if she doesn't keep him fed."

Isaac chuckled and wiggled his brows. "He is a big boy."

I rarely got embarrassed, but my grandfather's sexual innuendo managed to do it with ease. I knew exactly how big Zaedon was after spending a night in his arms, and being reminded about the size of his male parts was intimate enough to send heat to my cheeks. I glanced over my shoulder, searching for something, anything, to distract my grandfather. Spotting Zaedon, the object of my discomfort, rushing toward the vehicle didn't help.

"My apologies for the delay." Zaedon climbed inside and sat down next to me, possessively clutching the container Ellie had given him.

"No problem," Isaac said, then ran his hands over the controls, the engine rumbling to life. "Engine sounds great, Cara." He pressed on the accelerator, turning the vehicle toward the worn road that would take us to the backside of the fields.

"With any luck, you shouldn't have any more issues." My attention was on Derrick and the way he glared at Zaedon.

Derrick moved back into his original spot, then faced forward with his arms crossed when he noticed me frowning at him.

The tension between the two males was hard to miss. After about ten minutes of driving, I'd had enough and tapped my grandfather's shoulder. "Here works."

"Why are we stopping?" Zaedon glanced at me curiously after checking out the surrounding landscape, an area where a sparse number of plants grew around large boulders.

"Because you and I are going to pick plants where the harvester can't reach." I waited for my grandfather to slow the vehicle to a stop, then pushed off the bench and jumped to the ground through the open space on my side of the control area.

"I'll go and help Cara, if you'd rather continue riding." Derrick spoke for the first time since we'd left my grandparents' place. "You know, since it's hard work and you've never done a harvest before." His tone was laced with more venom than a snakkril's bite.

Zaedon handled the challenge better than I would have. Instead of tossing Derrick from the harvester like he deserved, he grinned. "I appreciate your concern, but *Cara's* offer was extended to me." Zaedon rose from his seat, his massive size forcing him to hunch over to keep from banging his head on the overhead canopy. "I am not afraid to work, and I am certain she can teach me whatever I need to know."

Even if there wasn't a bounty on my head, dividing my time between working for Burke and helping out in the farming community was never going to change. When I'd volunteered to help with the manual picking a week ago, I figured after a day of hard labor, Zaedon would decide he no longer wanted to be my bodyguard and return to the settlement.

After spending more time with him, waking up in his arms, then surviving the ordeal with the bandits, I viewed him differently and was regretting my decision to persuade him to leave.

On the other hand, if, after a hard day of work and our trip to the settlement to talk to Khyron, Zaedon decided not to return with me, I'd know the chemistry between us was a passing attraction, not something that might turn into a lasting relationship. Sadly, thinking about the possibility made me feel even worse.

Not in the mood to wait for the two males to stop glaring at each other, I pushed the unwanted thoughts aside, then waved at my grandfather and started walking.

\*\*\*

*Zaedon*

It had been obvious from the moment I was introduced to Derrick that he wanted Cara for himself. For all her intelligence and perceptive abilities, she seemed unable to comprehend his interest in her, or maybe she knew and pretended otherwise. I hoped it was the latter. Either way, I had lost my patience with the male and was ready to pummel him to ensure he understood I would not relinquish my claim on her.

Towering over him when I stood inside the limited space of the control and noticing his cringe gave me a little satisfaction.

"Zaedon." Isaac interrupted my thoughts and ended the intense glare I had aimed at Derrick.

I did my best not to snap at the older male. "Yes?"

"If you're planning on helping Cara, you might want to get going." He tipped his head to the left. "It doesn't look like she's going to wait for you."

Cara had already put some distance between the harvester and herself. I groaned, squeezing through the narrow exit, then jumped to the ground to race after her.

She did not slow her pace or acknowledge my presence. It was unclear if my behavior had angered her or if she was contemplating something else. "Cara." An apology seemed like a waste of words, since it was unclear what I would be apologizing for, so I decided to start a conversation on a safer subject. "If we are working manually, how do we gather what we harvest?"

The question brought a wry smile to her face. "You know what a grundogal is, right?"

I nodded. "I have never had the opportunity to interact with one, but I understand they are docile animals." The outlying regions on Ketaurrios were home to many creatures. There were some that interacted well with other inhabitants and some that were deadly and didn't.

"That's one way of putting it." She shifted the direction we were heading toward an outcropping of rock, the nearby sand covered with foot-high patches of reddish-orange grass. Beyond that was a wooden building no larger than a small storage area. "We use them to pull our wagons."

"Wagons?" It was a human term I was not familiar with.

"A large container on wheels." She walked around the building and pointed. "This is a wagon. The harness and rigging we use to attach it to the grundogal are inside the shed."

I helped her pull everything we needed from the building's interior, then watched her attach the rigging to the wagon. The process did not take long, but I had yet to see one of the animals we would need to assist us. "Where do we find one of your grundogals?"

"That's what this is for." She walked over to the shed, then returned with a long, narrow piece of handcrafted wood with tiny holes carved along one side. "Grab a clump of that grass over there and be ready."

"Be ready for what?" I asked as I walked over to the nearest patch and pulled a handful of the plant out of the ground. How difficult could it be to use the plant to lure a grundogal in the same manner my friends and I coerced a chaugwas for riding?

"You'll see." Cara held the small cylinder to her lips and blew. The shrill and annoying noise made me want to cover my ears. She took a seat on the end of the wagon, swinging her legs back and forth, patiently waiting.

A minute or so passed, then a similar sound blared in the distance. Not long after that, I heard a loud snorting noise coming from my right and turned to see a grundogal burst through an opening between two boulders. For a creature with short, wide legs, it moved rapidly. Its long body was covered with pale yellow scales, and its tail had a stubby appearance as if part of it had been chopped off, though I knew it hadn't.

"Oh, no, it's Chompers." She jumped to her feet.

"You gave the creature a name?" I shot her a disbelieving glance.

"I didn't name him. The children in the village did." She scowled at me, then back at the rapidly approaching creature. "You might want to get rid of the grass."

Her instructions did not make any sense, a fact I relayed with the confused look I shot at her. "Why would I…" I did not get to finish my question. Chompers had picked up his pace and did not appear to be slowing down or altering his course, which seemed to be aimed at me. I got a glimpse of broad, solid muscles right before he barreled into me and knocked me to the ground.

He shifted his weight across my upper body, then snatched the grass from my hand and started chewing. It was getting difficult to breathe, and no matter how much I shoved against his side with my free hand, the creature would not budge.

"Told you to get rid of the grass." Cara appeared by my head, hands on her hips, her smile beaming.

I was not amused, nor did I want to be chastised, not with Chompers's leg pressing heavily against my male parts. "A little help?" The words came out raspy.

"I don't know. It's not every day I get to see a mighty vryndarr taken down by a grundogal."

Glaring at her was not helping; neither was trying to get my left arm out from under Chompers. "Cara, please. I would like to continue breathing."

"I suppose if you're going to beg." She walked away, quickly returning with a handful of grass. "Come on, Chompers." She wiggled the long blades in front of his face, coaxing him to get off me. She dropped the remainder of the grass on the ground, then turned and held out her hand. "Better?"

"Much." I took her hand, and, instead of allowing her to help me up, I pulled her down on top of me, smiling when she squealed. I wrapped my arms around her waist, knowing she had the ability to escape whenever she wished and was glad that she did not try to push away. "I believe a better explanation about what to expect from a grundogal would have been helpful."

"I'm sorry." She giggled. "Chompers is still young, and he's the only one that does that."

If he was considered young, I wondered how large an adult would be.

"He also likes to lick with a lot of slobbering." She glanced toward Chompers, who had finished the grass she'd given him and was moving toward us. "So unless you want him on top of you again, we should get off the ground."

Chompers and I were going to have issues if he continued to interfere with my time with Cara. With a reluctant groan, I released her.

"Oh, and I was only kidding about the slobbering part." She laughed, strolling over to the wagon to grab the harness. "You'll also need these." She dug around in her bag and pulled out what appeared to be flat pieces of fabric, thicker than anything I had seen used for clothing, more like the hide from an animal.

"Your hands are pretty big, so I hope these fit."

"What are they?" I asked, curious to know why she was referring to my hands.

"They're called gloves, and they're designed to protect our hands while we work, keep our skin from getting blisters." She grabbed the larger two of the four pieces. "Now hold up your hand like this."

I followed her example, enjoying the feel of her skin caressing mine as she worked the material onto my hand. I was not used to wearing any kind of covering on my hands and was impressed at how well I could flex my fingers. "My hands are bigger than those of most human males. Where did you find these?" As far as I knew, there were not any ketaurrans living in the community.

"Do you remember me introducing you to Faith the day after we arrived?"

"The female with the three young ones?" I asked.

"Yeah. She's really good at making clothes, so I had her make these for you."

"You had someone prepare a gift...for me?"

"I guess you can call them a gift, if you want," she said.

"Thank you, Cara." I lifted her around the waist, brushing a soft kiss to her lips before returning her to the ground.

By her confused expression, I did not think she understood how much her thoughtful action had affected me. Had the gloves been given to me by someone else, I might not have felt as strongly about it.

"Okay." She drew out the word. "It's really no big deal. Everyone wears them during the harvest."

"Then we should get started." I flexed my fingers and grinned. "Show me what I need to do."

"Sure, just let me get Chompers hooked up to the wagon first."

After slipping a lead onto the animal's head, she handed it to me, then draped the harness over his back and attached the wagon.

"We'll start with the plants growing closest to the boulders." She led Chompers to an area near a clump of deep burgundy stalks that easily reached the middle of my thigh, then showed me how to extract the pods growing near the top without pulling out the roots and damaging the entire plant.

It was not long before we got into a comfortable, steady rhythm of systematically working one area before moving on to another. By the time we'd filled half of the wagon, and judging by the sun's location in the sky, it was late morning.

Cara wiped her hand across her brow. "I could use a break. How about you?"

I raised an inquiring brow. "Does this break include food?"

"I suppose now would be a good time to stop for lunch. There's a cool place near those rocks over there where we can eat." Cara grabbed her bag, along with the extra container of pyteinnas Ellie had given me.

I had been so occupied with helping Cara and enjoying my time with her that I had forgotten about them. We left Chompers to graze on some nearby grass and settled on the ground in a shady spot with our backs against the flattened side of some rocks.

I placed the container on my lap and took the water cylinder she handed to me. "Is picking the plants by hand your usual task?"

"Not always. Sometimes I ride on the harvester so I can spend more time with my grandfather." She opened the other container and took out a flat cake.

"Do you work every harvest?"

"I try to be here for as many as I can, but sometimes the jobs I do for Burke take longer than I'd like."

"Do Ellie and Isaac know how dangerous your work is?" I had been hungrier than I realized and quickly stuffed a second pyteinna into my mouth.

She took a long swallow of water. "They know I do things to help my people, but not the full extent."

"Do they mind when you are gone?" I asked.

"I know they miss me. They also understand that what I do is important, that I need my independence, and would never try to stop me." She studied me as if expecting a negative reaction to her comment.

I understood her need to be a warrior, to protect her people. Other than convincing her that she was my ketiorra and I wanted her in my life always, I would never try to persuade her to do something different.

"What about you? Have you always been a vryndarr?" Cara asked.

"Yes, since I was a young male. I trained with Jardun and Garyck. We traveled with the old drezdarr during the war." I missed the elder male and still grieved his death. I preferred to leave the memories of that horrible time in the past.

"Is that when you ended up with Khyron?"

I nodded, then reached for another cake. "The others and I have known him most of our lives. He is more than the ruler of our people, he is my family, my friend. Much like Laria, Celeste, and Sloane are for you."

The next few minutes of eating the remainder of our lunch were spent in comfortable silence. Though my time with Cara was extremely pleasurable, the issue surrounding the sabotage of the harvester part weighed heavily on my mind. There was no easy way to bring up the topic without causing her stress, but it was a conversation I needed to have with her while we were alone.

"Cara, we have not yet discussed who might have been responsible for tampering with the part on the harvester." There were several pyteinna left, so I resealed the container.

"Yeah, I've been wondering about that myself." She stuffed her half-drained water cylinder back into the bag. "I truly have no idea who it could be. Even if someone knew about the bounty and was after me, they'd have no reason to mess with the harvest, not unless they were okay with starving."

Someone knowing about the bounty was the most logical explanation, yet I could not shake the feeling that it might be something else. "You are familiar with the people here. Do you have any idea who might want to cause the vehicle, or you harm?" It would take more convincing for me to believe she had not been the target.

She leaned back against the rock, slumping her shoulders. "I've known the people here a long time, some of them when I lived aboard the *Starward Bounty*." She played with the strap on her bag. "Everyone here pretty much acts like one big family. Well, most everyone, anyway."

"Would Derrick happen to be on that list of not everyone?"

"I would say he falls somewhere in the middle," she said.

I had been suspicious of the male from the start, more because of his interest in Cara than anything else. Now I questioned whether or not my instincts had been trying to tell me something.

"I never cared for him much, but he was Graham's friend, so I learned to tolerate him."

"And now?" I skimmed her ankle with the tip of my tail.

She smiled. "I like him even less, but I'll continue to get along with him for Ellie and Isaac's sake. At least until he gives me a reason not to." She pretended to grab for my tail when I moved it to her thigh.

Frowning, I snatched it out of her reach. "Cara."

"Hmm?"

"I know you can take care of yourself, but promise me you will be more wary until we have time to uncover the truth."

"We?" Her dark eyes held mine. "Does that mean you're planning on coming back after we talk to Khyron?"

I shifted, taking her hand in mine. "Cara, you are…" I wanted to tell her she was my ketiorra, that I would never leave her. "No, I plan to return. I vowed to keep you safe and will continue to do so."

Shrill snorting, along with quickened movement, drew

my attention. Chompers was no longer content to graze where we had left him and was heading away from us with the wagon. I picked up my container and handed it to her before getting to my feet. "I fear our young friend is going to disappear with our harvest."

"I forgot to mention he also has a tendency to wander off." Cara laughed as she stuffed everything back in the bag. "It's a good thing we don't have much farther to go before we meet up with the others."

# CHAPTER NINE

*Cara*

The relief I felt after learning Zaedon wasn't leaving, that my plan to run him off hadn't worked, came with a small amount of exhilaration. Though his reason for staying centered on following orders, a part of me hoped there was more to it than simply keeping his promise to my friends and the drezdarr.

The more time I spent with him, the more he surprised me. He'd treated the gloves I'd given him as if they were a treasured prize. For an imposing warrior, his reaction to the simple gesture was adorable. Knowing his view on any description that didn't compliment his manhood, I refrained from saying anything and savored the moment.

He got even worse the first time juices from one of the pods he'd picked got on the material. It took me five minutes to convince him the juices would stain his skin, and that he needed to keep the gloves on, not tuck them in my bag to protect them.

Telling him I could always have another pair made was a big mistake. He'd clutched the gloves to his chest and glared at me as if I'd insulted him. Once they were on his

87

hands, they stayed there. The only time he'd taken them off was when we stopped for lunch.

I pulled the bag's strap onto my shoulder and walked over the area that still needed picking and watched Zaedon. He'd grabbed a handful of grass before chasing after Chompers, and was easily coaxing the animal to return with him.

"You've done this before, haven't you?" I asked, hooking the bag on the side of the wagon.

"The grundogal are not much different from a chaugwas, only smaller." He smiled, opening his hand and letting Chompers snatch the last few blades of grass from his palm.

"Celeste told me about having to ride them across the wastelands, and how she'd named hers Lou," I said.

Zaedon chuckled. "She seemed very sad when we had to leave him behind. I believe if she could have found a way to bring him with us, she would have."

A rumble filled the air, spooking Chompers. I grabbed his lead and ran my head along his neck to keep him calm and stop him from running off. In the distance, I spotted a minisolport, a smaller two-seater version of a solarveyor, heading toward us. "That can't be good," I muttered.

The lack of technological communication anywhere on the planet had always been a problem. One the engineers who'd survived the crash had no luck overcoming. Supposedly, there was something in the atmosphere that screwed with signals, and the erratic weather didn't help either.

In order to minimize any problems that might arise during a harvest, the agricultural experts, which included my grandparents, built roadways large enough for the solarveyors to travel around the fields. It didn't matter how much preparation was done ahead of time, there was always a chance something would go wrong.

As soon as the vehicle stopped, the access door opened and Derrick jumped to the ground and hurried toward us.

"Cara, we need you." He skidded to a stop a few feet away from me.

My pulse raced. My first concern was Isaac and whether something had happened to him. "What's wrong?"

"Your grandfather's harvester broke down. Josh tried to fix it, but I think he hurt his hand again. He might even need to have the breaks in his bones reset."

Anger replaced worry, and I snapped. "Why didn't he send for me first?" Josh could be stubborn sometimes. He liked to do things himself, hated to rely on others if he didn't have to. If he'd injured his hand again, I'd bet anything he was regretting his decision not to send someone for me sooner.

"I'm really to blame. I've been helping Josh out when you're not around and thought it would be an easy fix." He averted his gaze. "I may have made things worse."

I hated leaving any of the crop behind, but the quantity we'd lose if the harvester wasn't functioning was considerable compared to what was handpicked. Harvesting was an all-day event, which meant a long time with the main machines down was costly.

The mini was designed for hauling, but it would take too much time to unload the wagon's contents into the storage containers kept in the cargo area. I'd expected Zaedon to insist on coming with me, and for the first time, I was disappointed he didn't. I found myself searching for an excuse not to go without him.

"We can't just leave what we picked, and there's at least another half hour's worth of work to do."

"Why don't you take the transport back? I can stay and help Zaedon finish," Derrick offered, a little too enthusiastically.

"Cara, he is right. You should go and let us finish here." Zaedon reached for the lead in my hand.

My internal warning system was blaring, and after their interaction earlier, I wasn't sure leaving them alone together was such a good idea. Though Derrick's behavior seemed unusual, maybe I was worrying for nothing. He wasn't armed, at least not that I could see, and if something did happen, Zaedon was quite capable of taking care of himself.

Zaedon also had to be the most even-tempered male I'd ever met. I tried to convince myself this had more to do with completing the harvest and not my instincts telling me that leaving would be a mistake. Maybe I was worrying for nothing, and the uneasy flutter in my stomach was self-inflicted stress associated with getting the harvester back up and running.

Still unable to shake the feeling, I placed my palm on Zaedon's chest. "Are you sure you'll be okay?"

He covered my hand with his and smiled. "Repairing the harvester is important." He pressed a gentle kiss to my forehead. "Now, go. I will make sure to take care of these plants for you."

I noticed he hadn't mentioned Derrick in his promise to finish the task. There was no doubt Zaedon had done it on purpose to irritate him, and the way Derrick was glaring at him didn't make me feel any better about leaving. "Fine, but as soon as I'm done, I expect to find you at the meeting place with my grandfather." I turned and sprinted toward the mini.

\*\*\*

*Zaedon*

In the few weeks we had spent together, Cara had never requested my presence, let alone insist I meet her somewhere. I had wanted her to know that I trusted her and staying behind, though difficult, seemed to have been the right decision. I watched the transport until it was nothing more than a tiny spot in the distance. The farther away from me she moved, the heavier the pressure constricting my chest became.

When Derrick first arrived, and offered his help, something devious, bordering on malicious, flared in his dark eyes. Even the tone of his voice, which he had tried to disguise, led me to believe he had a hidden purpose behind his request to stay behind. A purpose I planned to discover now that Cara was safely on her way.

I ignored Derrick and led Chompers toward the nearest patch of plants and went back to work. Sometimes, when dealing with someone trying to be deceitful, remaining silent was the best way to draw out their intentions rather than questioning them directly.

Derrick was not armed, but he had come prepared to carry out his facade. He slipped on the pair of gloves he had tucked in his waistband, then began removing pods from the plants a few feet away from me. I only had to wait a few minutes before he stopped what he was doing to speak. "You know you don't stand a chance with her, right?"

I gripped a plant the way Cara had shown me and carefully extracted two more pods, then tossed them in the wagon. "Perhaps."

"Perhaps nothing. There's no way she'd ever be interested in someone like you." He tightened his jaw, red spreading across his cheeks.

I took a deep breath, ignoring his comment. It would do me no good to inform him that his inference about Cara sharing the same dislike for my people as he did was inaccurate. Besides the affection she bestowed on Torrlun and his family, she had shown nothing but respect for my friends and me.

Being a vryndarr and personal bodyguard to the drezdarr was a dangerous existence that did not come without sacrifices. Ketaurran males were expected to protect females. Although the females of my species were strong, they were not trained to fight. For many years, my friends and I believed we would spend our lives without a female by our sides. A belief that changed soon after we met the human females, the ones we considered warriors.

After Jardun discovered Laria was his ketiorra, his mate, I clung to the hope that I would someday find a female who was my equal. Now that I had found Cara, I was not going to let this human, or any other male, come between us.

The faraway rumble of a transport engine, growing steadily louder, interrupted our conversation. Cara was an excellent mechanic, but I struggled to believe she had repaired the harvester so quickly and was returning. My suspicions were confirmed when a midsize version of a solarveyor approached from the opposite direction she had taken.

Hearing the advancing vehicle, Chompers nervously jerked his head. I grabbed his lead and brushed his neck with gentle strokes as Cara had done earlier.

As soon as the vehicle stopped, a human male I did not recognize appeared in the open entryway, then jumped the short distance to the ground. "Looks like Mike's right on time." Derrick pulled off his gloves, smirking with satisfaction.

"Right on time for what?" I asked Derrick, feigning surprise since I already knew Derrick and his friend most likely meant me harm.

"To get you out of Cara's life and make sure you never come back." Derrick's confident warning lost impact, the last few words faltering. His eyes widened, seemingly unsettled by the appearance of a second male getting out of the transport.

The two males walked in our direction, Mike's strides lacking the confidence possessed by the second male. He nervously pushed his light brown hair off his forehead several times before he reached us. Compared to Derrick, he was of equal height, but he was wider, with extra weight around his hips and midsection.

The second male had long, dark hair tied at his nape,

and a scar running the length of his right forearm. His eyes possessed the unwavering intensity of a merc or someone who lived in their world. A sword the length of his thigh was strapped to his hip, and I had no doubt he had the ability to use it.

Mike glanced from me to his friend. "Derrick, I…"

"What's he doing here?" Derrick jutted his chin at the other male.

"Thought I'd collect the goods in person." He smirked, perusing me from top to bottom as if I was something on display at the trader's market. "A big ketaurran like him will fetch a nice price."

I was relieved that the male had no idea I was a vryndarr. Hearing he sold ketaurrans into slavery nauseated me and was reason enough to end his life. After watching Logan interrogate two of Doyle's males the previous month, I was more inclined to let him live and turn him over to Burke. If there was even a small possibility of finding the slavers and finally putting an end to their practices, I would gladly ensure he made it to the settlement alive.

Derrick grabbed his friend's arm, as if pulling him a few feet away would keep the other male or me from overhearing what he had to say. "This is not what we discussed. You were just supposed to show up and leave." He warily glanced at the merc. "What if someone sees him? What if Cara comes back before…" He roughly swiped his hand through his hair, then rubbed his nape.

"If you misaligned the connectors in the harvester like we talked about, then Cara will be too busy with the repair and you won't have anything to worry about," Mike said.

Getting Cara to leave before Derrick's friend and the merc arrived was the only part of his plan I was thankful for. If the merc was also in the business of collecting bounties and realized who she was, her life would have been in danger. So far, Derrick seemed unaware of the reward, his feelings for Cara the only motivation for wanting me gone.

Derrick's nervous gaze shot to the empty road behind us. "I guess you're right."

Mike smacked Derrick's arm with the back of his hand. "Of course, I am."

With the additional support from his friend, Derrick got a little braver and glared at me. "This is your own fault."

Chompers had calmed and was sniffing the ground searching for more grass. I released his lead and crossed my arms. "How so?" I was curious to hear his reasoning.

"If you'd gotten hurt and left after I sabotaged the harvester, then I wouldn't have had to find another way to get rid of you."

I curled my fingers into my arms, tamping down the urge to punch the male repeatedly. "Did you even consider what would have happened if Cara had been the one who touched the part and not me?"

"Well, no, I…" Derrick's face paled, the reality of what could have happened registering. "No, that's not possible. I saw you two working together. She always had you help with the connectors, so I knew it would be you." His voice wavered, his justification lacking conviction.

I removed my gloves, unwilling to get blood on the gift Cara had given me. And blood would spill, the amount depending on the merc's skill level and how long it took me to disarm him. "What excuse are you planning to give Cara when she discovers I am gone?"

Doubt flickered in his eyes. Clearly, he had not given the outcome of my disappearance any thought.

Mike chimed in. "Don't you worry, we'll think of something."

"We had a deal, so don't even think about changing your mind." The merc spoke to Derrick, then withdrew his sword. "Now, let's get this over with so I can get out of here."

Cara's explanation of my continued stay in the

community was based on partial truths. The humans were led to believe I was here at the request of the drezdarr to deter a recent increase in bandit activity, my true identity kept secret even from her grandparents. Many of the village's inhabitants would be working the harvest. I was afraid showing up visibly armed might intimidate some of them and had chosen to leave my blades in my room.

The only weapon available was the thin dagger Cara had given me during our escape from the bandits. I had tucked it inside my boot, intent on returning it to her later. Even without the use of a blade, disarming and incapacitating the three males equated to a workout with little or no challenge.

Since the merc was the only one with a weapon, he must have thought I could be easily controlled. He aimed the tip of his blade in my direction. "Get in the transport."

"And if I choose not to comply?" I moved away from Chompers and the wagon, giving myself more room to maneuver.

"Then I'm afraid this is going to get bloody." He swiped the blade back and forth through the air. "Because one way or another, you're leaving with me."

I had noticed that most of the people living in the farming community did not use weapons, which included Derrick and Mike. I was fairly certain they possessed limited fighting skills and was not surprised when they took a few steps back.

Just because they had chosen not to participate did not mean I would dismiss them as a threat. They must have had something else in mind for disabling me when they had devised their plan to turn me over to the merc. I concentrated on the male with the blade, but made sure not to let Mike and Derrick get behind me.

"I believe you are mistaken." I dodged his first two swipes.

I would have to get close in order to disarm him, a necessary tactic, one that greatly increased my chances of sustaining an injury. I advanced an intimidating step forward. The male held his position and swung again. The tip of his blade grazed my skin, leaving a thin cut and blood trickling along my arm.

"Told you it was going to get bloody." He smirked and prepared for another strike.

Mike had not moved, but now that I had sustained a wound, Derrick appeared to be a little braver and was inching to my right. A growl and a quick angry glare from me stopped his progress.

The longer I took to disarm the male, the greater the chances that Cara would return. Having her fight by my side was not the issue. It was having the merc recognize her and say something about it in front of Mike and Derrick. They could, in turn, repeat it to someone in the community who wouldn't have a problem turning her in for Doyle's bounty. It would also increase the chances of her grandparents finding out about the dangerous and life-threatening work she did for Burke. The things she tried so hard to protect them from.

This time when he swung with his blade, I sidestepped instead of moving backward. As soon as the sharp metal tip passed my chest, I grabbed his arm.

When he tried to wrench free, I brought up my knee, smashing his wrist against my thigh. The crackle of bone snapping filled the air. The male howled in pain and dropped his blade.

He staggered backward, clutching his damaged arm to his chest. "You draecking lizard, you broke my arm!" His seething gaze went from me to his sword. "Screw the reward. One less ketaurran on the planet is fine by me." He dove for the blade, landing in the dirt on his stomach, his fingers inches from the handle.

I was faster, snatching it off the ground before he could reach it, then punching his jaw, knocking him out and guaranteeing he stayed in an unconscious state for a long time.

I quickly got to my feet and glared at the other two males, the majority of my anger directed at Derrick. "Who is next?" I cracked my neck, then swiped the blade through the air. Unless they lacked the intelligence to know they would not win, I had no intention of harming either of them.

Mike, wide-eyed and pale faced, jerked his head from the unmoving merc to me. He swallowed hard, then slowly started backing away.

"Mike, where do you think you're going?" Derrick asked when his friend continued to put distance between them.

"I'm getting out of here." He turned and ran toward the transport, muttering, "I didn't sign up for dying" as he went.

Out of the three males, Derrick was the one I held accountable for what had transpired. I was determined to make him pay for inadvertently trying to harm Cara. Going after Mike would divide my attention and give Derrick a chance to flee.

I could have used the dagger in my boot to stop Mike, but there was no honor in knifing the male from behind. After switching the merc's blade to my other hand, I bent over and selected a rock large enough to fit in my palm, then threw it using the same accuracy I applied to my blades.

"Mike, look out!" Derrick's warning did no good.

The rock caught Mike between the shoulder blades, pushing him into the transport, his head bouncing off metal. With a loud groan, he toppled sideways, landing in the sandy dirt, gripping his head and moaning.

I turned to Derrick, giving him the scowl he deserved. "This ends now unless you would like to end up like your friend."

# CHAPTER TEN

*Cara*

The longer it took me to reach Zaedon, the more irritated I got. I let up on the accelerator just enough to maneuver the transport around one of the larger ruts in the road, but not enough to keep it from bouncing across the uneven surface.

I couldn't believe Derrick had lied to me, and as soon as I found out why, I was going to hurt him. The level of pain he'd suffer depended on whether or not I found Zaedon in the same condition I'd left him.

The damage to the harvester was a simple connector repair, a fix I was able to make in less than ten minutes. It would've been easy for Derrick to tamper with the engine undetected while everyone was preoccupied during the lunch break.

So, not only had what he'd told me about the harvester being in bad shape been untrue, but his story about Josh hurting his hand had been a total fabrication. During harvests, everyone in the community found a way to contribute to the process. Since Josh couldn't pick plants or assist with repairs, he'd volunteered to help with the transports that delivered additional water and food throughout the day. When Derrick concocted his make-believe story to get me away from Zaedon, he hadn't counted on Josh showing up shortly after I arrived to fix the problem with the harvester.

"Draeck, Cara," Josh cursed. "I'd like to get there without breaking any more bones." Minis were designed to carry two people. With Isaac sitting in the seat next to me, Josh had been forced to sit in the open cargo area behind us.

I glanced between the seats where Josh sat, brows furrowed, green eyes glaring, gripping the structural bar running horizontally along the wall with his good hand. His long legs were bent at the knees so he'd fit in the narrow space between the storage bins stacked against the opposite wall. "Sorry." I slowed the vehicle a little more, then sped up a few minutes later when the road evened out again.

"Cara, I'm sure Zaedon's fine. He seems like the kind of male who can handle himself in any situation." Isaac held the edge of the control panel with a white-knuckled grip since the minis didn't have safety straps to keep people in their seats. He hadn't been any happier to hear what Derrick had said than Josh had been, and, after assigning someone else the task of harvesting the last small area had insisted he come along with us.

The rational part of my mind agreed with my grandfather. It was the irrational, emotional part, the part that understood how devastated I'd be if something terrible had happened to Zaedon, that disagreed.

I gripped the steering control tighter, wishing I'd listened to my instincts, and notched the accelerator up higher, taking the final turn in the road too fast. As soon as I rounded the final curve and saw a solarveyor parked in the middle of the roadway, my feeling of dread went from tingling along my spine to tearing through my system.

"Isaac, any idea who that transport belongs to?" I was

familiar with the vehicles in the village since I'd worked on most of them at one time or another.

"No, never seen it before."

"Me neither." Josh knelt between the seats now that he wasn't being bounced around in the back anymore.

I geared down the engine, bringing the vehicle to a stop a few feet away from the other transport. There was no sign of anyone anywhere. No Zaedon, no Derrick, no Chompers and the wagon, and certainly no one who could have arrived in the transport.

My heart raced, the pressure in my chest so tight, I could hardly breathe. All I could think about was finding Zaedon, and wondered what condition he'd be in when I did.

I'd barely given the access panel on my side of the vehicle a chance to open before I was sliding out and rushing around the other vehicle. I froze after nearly tripping over a pair of long legs belonging to a human male I didn't recognize. His wrists and ankles were bound, his upper body braced against the transport. His eyes were closed, and his head lolled to one side. There was a red blotch along one side of his chin, evidence that he'd been punched.

"Damn, do you think Zaedon did that?" Josh asked, stopping on my left and staring at the male on the ground.

"Of course he did." Isaac moved to my other side. "Told you the boy could take care of himself, same as my baby girl here," he stated proudly.

"Yeah, but if Zaedon did this, then where is he?" I stuck my head through the open doorway of the solarveyor, knowing I'd be unable to relax until I actually saw him. "And where's Derrick?" I asked after finding it empty.

"I think I know." Josh walked past the other end of the transport and pointed to an area farther down the road.

I stepped around the male on the ground to get a better look and saw Zaedon coaxing Chompers with a handful of grass. I got a glimpse of Derrick and another male a short distance behind him.

Relieved he was okay, I took off running, not bothering to wait for my grandfather and Josh. "Zaedon," I called out when I got closer.

Zaedon snapped his head in my direction, a wide grin on his face. "Cara, I presume the repair went well."

"The harvester is up and running." I couldn't believe he was asking about the repair when I was more interested in the bound and unconscious male propped against the transport. I didn't stop walking until I was less than a foot away from him. "You're okay?" It was more of a question than a statement.

"I am." Zaedon placed his hands on my hips, pulling me closer. "Why would I not be?"

I pressed my palms to his chest, the physical contact relaxing me even more. "Because there's a male on the ground back there, and I thought you might have been…" I noticed the cut and drying blood on his arm. "Wait, you're hurt." I touched the skin below his injury.

He glanced at his arm and shrugged. "It is nothing."

I heard a loud cough and glanced behind me at Josh and Isaac. Josh quickly hid a smirk, and my grandfather's grin got even wider. Zaedon, the frustrating male, must have seen them approach, knew they were standing there listening, but hadn't bothered to say anything. He'd also slipped his tail around the backs of my legs so I couldn't pull away easily.

"Glad to see you're okay," Isaac said.

"Yeah, Cara was concerned about you," Josh added with an amused smile.

Zaedon raised a brow. "She was?"

The glare I leveled at Josh meant there'd be retribution if he told Zaedon just how badly I'd overreacted. "Maybe just a little." I squirmed so Zaedon would let me go, then stepped back to face all three of them. "I want to know what happened after I left." I had some theories, but I wanted to hear the details from Zaedon.

"Cara, I can explain." Derrick had stopped picking and was rushing toward us.

One glimpse and I recognized the male tagging closely behind Derrick. His name was Mike, and he didn't live in the village. He was a regular visitor and spent most of his time hanging out with Derrick. I also noticed that neither male wore gloves, their hands stained a vibrant purplish blue from picking pods, no doubt Zaedon's idea.

"Good." I poked Derrick's chest. "Then start by telling me why you lied to me." Now that I'd had a chance to calm down and could think clearly, I realized he must have been the one who'd sabotaged the part Torrlun repaired. "After that, you can explain why you purposely damaged a part in the harvester so Zaedon and I had to drive all the way to Golyndier to get it repaired."

I could feel the heat rising on my cheeks, my state of lessened stress quickly disappearing. Thinking about our near miss with the mercs and our run-in with the bandits only irritated me more.

I took a deep breath, holding up my hand to let Derrick know I wasn't finished. "Most of all, I want to know why there's a merc lying on the ground over there"—I jabbed my thumb over my shoulder—"and why Zaedon has a blade wound on his arm." Since I'd never seen Derrick or Mike handle a blade, I assumed the sword strapped to Zaedon's waist had come from the unconscious male and was the cause of his injury.

At the sound of Mike's gasp, my glare jumped from Derrick to him. "Yeah, I know what he is, and I'm pretty sure I know what he's doing here."

"Better yet, since you're incapable of telling the truth and can't be trusted, I'd like to hear what Zaedon has to say first," Isaac said.

"You can't possibly…" Derrick stammered.

Isaac crossed his arms, silencing Derrick with a narrow-eyed glare. Anyone who'd ever dealt with my grandfather knew better than to argue with him when he gave that look, including me.

Derrick clamped his lips together, a flush darkening his cheeks.

Isaac tipped his head at Zaedon. "Why don't you tell us what happened?"

Zaedon glanced in my direction as if answering would somehow hurt me. I nodded, letting him know that the truth, no matter how unpleasant, was what everyone needed to hear.

"Derrick did not approve of my relationship with Cara and enlisted the services of a merc who planned to sell me into slavery." Zaedon's annoying arrogance appeared in his grin. "The male was foolish enough to believe I would go with him willingly, and learned otherwise."

I swallowed against the bile threatening to rise up my throat. What Derrick and Mike planned to do to Zaedon went way beyond despicable.

I'd never trusted Derrick, but he was part of the community and spent a great deal of time working with Josh and sometimes my grandfather. It bothered me even more to see the disappointment on their faces.

Contacting a merc took time. Derrick and Mike must have concocted their plan shortly after Zaedon arrived. More troubling was that they'd brought him to the community, to our home, and put the lives of all the families living here at risk.

Mercs rarely traveled alone. How long would it take for his friends to realize something had happened to him and decide to come looking for him?

If Derrick planned to have the merc get rid of Zaedon, he probably didn't know about the bounty on my head or that his actions would make it impossible for me to stay here any longer.

The more I thought about his betrayal, the angrier I got. "How could you do something so horrible, and why would you want to?"

"Because I care about you, Cara." He stretched out his hand, taking another step closer. "I couldn't let you choose him over me. His kind is responsible for the war. For so many deaths."

I didn't know if Derrick heard Zaedon's low snarl or realized what would happen to him if he touched me. As it was, I'd had enough of his narrow-minded thinking, and if Zaedon didn't get to him first, I was tempted to hurt him myself.

I sidestepped, moving between the two males. "Zaedon isn't responsible for the war or for what Sarus did to our people. In case you've forgotten, many ketaurrans died trying to protect us." I clenched my fists, tamping down the urge to do more than punch him. "So, yes, I would choose him over any male on the planet who thinks the way you do."

"Zaedon, I can't tell you how sorry I am that this happened." The glare my grandfather leveled at Derrick and Mike had them averting their gazes.

"Isaac, it is not your fault, nor do I hold you or anyone else in the community responsible." Zaedon seemed to be handling the whole situation a lot better than me.

My grandfather pursed his lips and scratched his chin contemplatively before addressing Derrick. "Do you have any idea what you've done? Either of you?" His stern gaze jumped to Mike. They must have understood that Isaac wasn't looking for an answer and complied by remaining silent.

"Not only did you hinder the harvest and jeopardize everyone's food supply, you breached the safety of the community. The mercs have never bothered us, and we can't let this one leave, not after what he's done. When his friends find out he's missing, there will be consequences." He rubbed his nape. The weight of the decision he was about to make showed in the deepened wrinkles around his eyes and the tightness in his jaw.

"I'm afraid the punishment for what you've done will

be severe." My grandfather turned to Zaedon. "Because you're the one they wronged, you have the right to choose the manner in which they are disposed of."

"Disposed of?" Mike's voice rasped, and he grabbed Derrick's arm. "What does that mean?"

Derrick shrugged him off. "Figure it out for yourself. You're the one who decided to change our plans and bring the merc here, not me."

I knew my grandfather, knew the hard decisions he'd had to make in the past. Once he learned that Derrick was responsible for sabotaging the harvester and knowingly put my life at risk, I knew there would only be one punishment. Hearing it voiced out loud solidified the reality of the situation, and I cringed. Derrick knew as well, yet he acted as if no one would dare hold him accountable.

Zaedon quietly pondered the decision. His gaze went from the defiant sneer on Derrick's face to the pale, wide-eyed shock on Mike's before finally giving my grandfather his answer. "The war took many lives, and though the drezdarr is working to unite the humans and the ketaurrans, order still needs to be maintained. Choosing whether or not to be merciful in this case is a decision I would prefer to leave with you and the other families they have wronged."

I had a feeling if things had gone differently and someone I cared about had gotten hurt, Zaedon's suggestion might have been different. The war had taught all of us that survival was hard, and kicking them out of the community, letting them leave, would be a mistake. If they were capable of bringing a merc here, they couldn't be trusted not to seek revenge and encourage others to attack our home.

The people living here might be healing from the wounds of losing friends and family members, but the memories were too fresh. They had a lot to lose, and mercy was going to take a long time to achieve. It definitely wasn't going to happen in this situation.

"I appreciate your candor and will pass the advice on to the other families." My grandfather turned to Josh. "Why don't you go and see if there is something in the solarveyor to bind them?"

"Sure." Josh didn't look pleased about the situation either, but stalked toward the vehicle anyway.

Tension filled the air the few minutes he was gone. When Josh returned, he had a set of shackles dangling from each hand. "Looks like the merc came prepared. These were sitting on the floor near the doorway." He handed a set to Isaac, then walked over to Derrick.

"Hands out, gentlemen." When Derrick and Mike refused to comply, my grandfather added, "Unless you want me to borrow Zaedon's sword and show you how well I can wield it."

Derrick had seen my grandfather handle a blade before, knew he was skilled, and didn't hesitate to hold out his wrists. Mike was a little more reluctant until Zaedon unstrapped the sword and handed it to my grandfather. With an appreciative nod, Isaac strapped the blade to his waist. "Josh and I will take them back in the transport and leave the mini here for you."

Once their wrists were cuffed, Josh motioned for them to move. "Let's go."

I watched Derrick drag his feet as Josh urged him and Mike toward the transport. He paused before climbing inside. Rage, disgust, and fear showed in the last glance he gave me.

"What about the merc?" I asked.

"We'll take him with us." Isaac spoke to Zaedon. "I don't suppose you'd mind helping Josh get him inside while I talk to Cara for a minute?"

"Not at all." Zaedon turned to follow Josh.

Isaac tucked a curl behind my ear. "Are you going to be okay?"

"Yeah." I nodded, not sure if I was being entirely truthful. Thinking I'd lost Zaedon had reminded me of the past.

"He's not Graham, you know." My grandfather's perception into what I was thinking always amazed me. "That boy was reckless and might have gotten you killed as well." He squeezed my hand. "Baby girl, don't look so surprised. I know what you do for Burke is dangerous, have known for a long time. So does Ellie."

"But you never said anything. Why?" I'd been so careful to keep the details of what I did a secret and couldn't believe they knew.

He smiled. "Figured there were a lot of things you couldn't share, so we never asked."

"Thanks for understanding."

"No problem." He scratched his chin. "You know I leave giving advice up to Ellie, but since she's not here, I wouldn't be much of a grandfather if I didn't tell you what we both think."

In other words, Ellie had been discussing me with him. Sharing his thoughts now wouldn't necessarily spare me from the lecture I could expect from her when I got back to the house. I'd found when dealing with my grandmother, it was always best to be prepared. I shook my head and groaned. "Fine, let's have it."

"Ellie thinks you should leave the past where it belongs and give Zaedon a chance."

"And she's the only one who feels that way?" I scrutinized him with a grin.

"Well, to be honest, she's not the only one. Clearly, the boy adores you and…" He glanced at something behind me. "Just think about it" was the last thing he said before Zaedon appeared at my side.

"The males are secured, and Josh is waiting for you," Zaedon said.

"I can send someone else to finish up if you both want a break," Isaac said.

With everything that had happened, I'd forgotten about Chompers. I glanced toward the last place I'd seen him, glad to see he'd found a large patch of grass and hadn't wandered off. "Since we're not far from the drop-off, Zaedon and I can unload the wagon and transport the storage bins." I turned to Zaedon. "If that's okay with you?"

He grinned. "I would very much like to finish what we started."

"You might want to take care of that cut on Zaedon's arm before too long." Isaac sauntered toward the transport, calling back at us as he walked, "Wouldn't want it to get infected."

"See, I'm not the only one who thinks we should take care of it now." Zaedon might argue with me, but he wouldn't argue with my grandfather. "There should be a medical kit in the mini."

Zaedon gently grabbed my hand. "Cara, it can wait."

Zaedon had proven more than once that he could take care of himself, that he'd willingly risk his life if it meant saving mine. I didn't have time to tell Isaac that his advice, though appreciated, was already too late. That I'd fallen for Zaedon in a big way and had already decided to give him a chance if he wanted to take one.

My position on not having a partner might have changed, but my stand on taking care of his wound hadn't. Conditions on the planet were harsh, and not addressing injuries in a timely manner could sometimes be fatal. I wasn't about to let Zaedon's passive attitude about the cut on his arm make him a casualty. "Zaedon, I'm sure you're right, but I want to do this." Then in a lower voice I said, "I need to do this."

# CHAPTER ELEVEN

*Zaedon*

Even if it was not in the context I had hoped for, I was elated when Cara came to my defense and stated that she would choose me over any other male. It was not easy dealing with the emotions that accompanied the realization that someone you knew could so blatantly betray your trust and that of the people you cared for. I'd resisted the urge to pull her into my arms, unsure if she would allow me to comfort her.

She was a strong female, not easily broken, but hearing the raspy tone in her voice when she pleaded for me to let her tend my wound was nearly my undoing.

When she went to retrieve the medical kit from the minisolport, I went after Chompers and coaxed him closer.

"Make yourself comfortable," she said, motioning to a nearby boulder.

Instead of sitting on the rock as she had intended, I sat on the ground with my back pressed against the hard surface, then took her hand and pulled her down with me.

She made a noise between a snort and a giggle and settled on my lap by straddling my legs. "Not exactly what

I meant, but I guess it'll work." She set the small rectangular kit between us and extracted what she needed to clean my wound.

She didn't look up until she'd meticulously wiped away all the dried blood. "If I didn't think you'd get all smug about it, I tell you the cut doesn't look bad."

I struggled not to grin. "Then I guess it is a good thing that you are not going to tell me."

She ignored my comment and retrieved a tiny container filled with a healing salve made from plants. After smearing it along the cut, she reached for a roll of fabric to use as a binding. "I'd hoped I'd be able to spend another day or two with my grandparents." She concentrated on wrapping the thin strip of material around my forearm several times before securing the ends. "After what I learned from Des, and now this thing with the merc, I think it would be a good idea to leave for the settlement tomorrow." She raised her head, locking her dark, inquiring gaze with mine.

"It is probably best. Maybe Burke has received more news and can give us an update on the situation with Doyle." I did not want Cara to spend the rest of her life worrying about the male's bounty and the danger it posed for her family. I was tempted to go after the male myself, but planned to have a private discussion with Khyron first to see what could be done to help her.

"All finished." She returned the supplies to the kit.

No sooner had we gotten to our feet than a shrill noise echoed around us. The sound was similar to the one made by the tubular stick Cara had used to summon a grundogal. Cara dropped the kit on the ground and quickly grabbed Chompers's lead. "Hold on a second," she said when the animal pranced back and forth, tugging to get away from her.

"That sounded like another animal from his herd, most likely his mother." She continued holding his lead and used her other hand to unhook one of the straps attached to the wagon. "Would you mind unhooking the other side? It shouldn't take us long to empty the wagon into the containers in the back of the mini, then take them to the meeting point to be unloaded."

As soon as the straps were removed, she slipped the lead off Chompers's head and stepped back. Without any encouragement, the creature took off in the direction of the other grundogal.

"I was just getting used to all the licking." I had grown fond of the animal and hated to see him go.

"I'm sure Chompers would be happy to give you some more of his slobbery kisses if you showed up to work the next harvest cycle," Cara teased.

"Would you be happy as well?" I grabbed her hips and pulled her closer.

"Maybe." She placed her hands on my shoulders.

"Happy enough to give me one of your slobbery kisses now so I will not miss Chompers so much?"

As expected, she huffed indignantly and smacked my chest. "I do not slobber."

I slipped my arms around her waist when she tried to pull away. "Unless you are willing to prove otherwise, I have not tasted your lips enough to know if you are telling the truth."

"You unbelievably arrogant…"

I captured her mouth with mine before she had a chance to finish, and was rewarded with a pleasurable moan. She slipped her hands to the back of my neck, then possessively took over the kiss, proving she could win the playful challenge I had set. Both of us were breathless by the time I found the strength to release her.

"Sooo." She stayed within the circle of my arms, giving me a satisfied smirk. "Did I slobber?"

"I am undecided." I slowly swept my tongue across my lower lip. "Perhaps I will need to do more testing to be sure."

"No more testing." She groaned and squirmed out of

my arms. "It will be dark soon, and we still need to unload the wagon."

\*\*\*

*Cara*

"I don't believe it." I smacked the flat metal surface next to the mini's controls.

"What is wrong?" Zaedon asked.

The mini's operating area lacked the room of a regular solarveyor, and he looked uncomfortable sitting in the passenger seat with his knees pressed against the control panel.

"There isn't enough power in the solars to make it back to my grandparents' place. It's too far to walk, so it looks like we're spending the night out here." The solars would automatically start charging as soon as the sunlight touched the panels on the roof, and we'd have enough power to make it home.

"Will Isaac send someone when we do not return to the village?" he asked.

After Isaac's earlier comment about me giving Zaedon a chance, I was pretty sure my grandparents wouldn't have a problem with me spending a night alone with him. They'd go out of their way to make sure no one came looking for us.

"I doubt it." I reached behind the seat and opened a small storage unit. "By the time they get done unloading the harvesters and storing what was picked, it will be late. Besides, he knows I can take care of myself, and he's convinced you can handle yourself in any situation."

"And you know about his thoughts how?" It was obvious by the tone of his voice that he was curious to know if Isaac had said anything to me about him.

If Zaedon was hoping for my grandparents' approval, he didn't need to worry. They'd thought he was wonderful ten minutes after meeting him, which, now that I'd had time to think about it, was why they'd encouraged me to spend more time with him. Not that I'd had a choice since I was the real reason he'd come to the farming community to begin with. "Um, he might have mentioned it during our drive earlier."

"This would be when you were concerned about my welfare, correct?"

Ignoring the infuriating male and the way he happily clung to the information I'd divulged, I continued to sift through the bin's items until I found what I was looking for.

"It's a good thing all the transports are stocked with emergency supplies." I pulled out a large bag, peeled back the flap, and dug through the contents. "It looks like there's a couple of blankets and some solar emitters in here."

"At least we won't starve." I got out of the vehicle, then reached inside to grab the bag sitting on the floor between the seats, the one containing water cylinders and what was left of our lunch. "Unless you ate the last of the pyteinna while I was gone."

Zaedon snorted. "It was difficult, but I resisted the urge to deplete our supplies." He stretched his body after removing himself from the cramped space. "Surely you are aware that I am a large male and require a lot of nourishment."

"I thought you ate so much because you enjoyed Ellie's cooking."

"There is that as well." He walked around the front of the vehicle and held out his hand, offering to take one of the bags. "Though, now that I am aware of your food preparation skills…"

"Don't even think about it. I'm not spending hours in the kitchen just so you can eat."

His laughter was infectious, and I couldn't stop smiling until I heard what sounded like rumbling in the distance. I glanced at the clear sky, noting the fading sunlight and straining to listen.

Zaedon heard it too and frowned at the skyline. "A storm is coming. Sleeping on the ground will not be possible."

Heavy rains could be brutal, and I preferred staying dry. "Guess we'll have to sleep in the back of the mini." I walked to the rear of the vehicle and opened the door. After setting my bag off to the side, I reached for a container.

Zaedon placed his hand on my arm to stop me. "If we leave the harvest outside, the rain will damage the contents."

"Most likely, but I don't think we have a choice. Getting caught in a downpour can be dangerous, and there's nothing else we can use for shelter."

"I have a better idea." He picked up the bag I'd discarded and waited for me to close the doors. "While you were repairing the harvester, I noticed the entrance to a cave." He took my hand and urged me toward the rocky formations a short distance away. "It is not ideal, but will protect us if it storms during the night."

"What if there's something already living in the cave, something unfriendly and not interested in sharing?" The planet had quite a few creatures, most with sharp claws, that liked living under the sandy dirt or in dark places.

"I am not worried. I have you to protect me."

Anticipating my reaction, he sidestepped to avoid a punch to his arm, then made it worse by laughing.

When Zaedon suggested spending the night in a cave, I didn't know we'd be climbing up an incline over several large boulders to reach the entrance. He'd insisted I go first so he could catch me if I slipped. I was pretty sure after glancing back and catching him staring at my backside that his motives had nothing to do with being heroic.

Shortly after we reached the ledge near a dark opening

that Zaedon would have to crouch to move through, he set the bags on the ground and dug out two of the glow emitters. After handing one to me, he held up his light and peered inside. "It is not as big as I had hoped, but it will protect us from any bad weather."

Once he made it into the cave without being attacked by something vicious, I crawled in behind him. "At least there's nothing with claws and fangs living in here." I aimed the light at all the corners, checking for anything that moved, I knelt on the hard, mostly even ground next to him. "I don't see any crognats, so that's a plus."

Crognats were tiny pale gold creatures that liked cool, dark places. They resembled something between an Earth beetle and a miniature lizard. Personally, I thought they were nothing more than a nuisance unless they decided to use their stinger. The tiny jab usually caused a painful red welt that lingered for several days.

I set the emitter on the ground and pulled the blankets out of the bag.

After helping me spread out one of the blankets, Zaedon sat with his long legs stretched out along one end, then smiled at me expectantly.

"You're hungry again, aren't you?"

"Looking after you is hard work." He grinned, leaning back and bracing his upper body with his arms.

"You mean keeping an eye on my backside is a lot of work, don't you?"

"I will have to admit it is a very nice backside."

"Uh-huh." The bag containing our food sat on the other side of him, and, instead of asking him to hand it to me, I reached over him.

He didn't bother to hide the sniff he took of my shoulder before I returned to my side of the blanket.

Zaedon had never lied to me, had always been honest in all our conversations. Thinking about Erin's advice, I decided now was a good time to ask him why he was constantly sniffing me. "Is there a reason you keep smelling me? I've taken plenty of baths since we got back from the Quaddrien, and I know I don't smell like chaugwas dung anymore."

"I know, and I have enjoyed smelling you after all of them." The turquoise in his eyes darkened.

"But why?"

Zaedon straightened, indecision furrowing his brow. "Because it is how a ketaurran male discovers the identity of"—he twirled the end of one of my curls around his finger—"his ketiorra."

"What?" I drop back on my haunches. "Are you saying that I... No, that can't be." I was self-assured in most instances, had no problem handling the toughest of situations, yet after hearing his claim, I couldn't form a simple sentence.

I took a deep breath and tried again. "Are you sure?"

"I am quite sure."

Not only did he just confirm there was definitely something between us, he'd also informed me I was his life mate. "How long have you known?"

"Since the day we arrived in Aztrashar."

"After I'd taken a bath." It was the day after we'd escaped from the Quaddrien, and I'd finally been able to wash off the dirt and stink I'd used as part of my disguise. I remembered how much I'd enjoyed soaking for over an hour.in the large tub carved out of stone

My pulsed raced, and I gripped the strap on the bag, trying to deal with the emotions pulsing through me. At the moment, anger was taking the lead. "Why didn't you tell me?"

"Human females, more specifically those with fighting skills, view things differently than ketaurran females. I was unsure of your reaction, feared you would leave, and I would never see you again." He dropped his hand to his lap.

I crossed my arms. "Then why keep it from me after you escorted me here?"

"You seemed unhappy about my presence and unwilling to accept my help. I did not want to fail at convincing you that we belong together." After a long pause, he caressed the side of my thigh with his tail. "Please tell me I have not ruined things between us."

This was the first time he'd openly admitted he cared for me and allowed me to glimpse his vulnerability. His motivations for not telling me had been sincere. I wondered how much of what I'd told him about losing Graham had been factored into his decision. I cared about him, wanted to be with him, and wasn't about to let him think otherwise.

I also wasn't going to disappoint him by surrendering too easily. I exaggerated a sigh, then speculatively tapped my chin. "You've already proven you're handy to have around in dangerous situations." I forced myself not to grin when he narrowed his gaze. "You're also not bad to look at, so that helps."

"Cara," he growled, then pulled me onto his lap so I straddled his thighs.

I draped my arms over his shoulders. "What?" I bit my lower lip, trying hard not to grin. "If I'm going to be your ketiorra, I want to know what I'm getting into."

"What else would you like to know?" Zaedon pulled me closer, the hard evidence of how much I affected him pressing against the sensitive spot between my legs.

He knew me better than I thought. By letting me lead and take control of the situation, he was showing me he understood what I needed. Thinking back on all his actions since I'd met him, he'd always supported my decisions. Sure, there'd been a few times when he argued with me, but he never once tried to force me to do something I didn't want to.

"I believe you said something about convincing me we belonged together. I'm curious to hear what you had in mind."

He ran his hand along my back, stopping to tangle his

fingers in the hair at my nape. "I would start by disproving my notion that you slobber."

"I thought we already..." He stopped me from talking with a kiss. A kiss that started out slow and enticing, then gradually progressed to possessively dominating. I responded by rubbing my body against him, wanting and needing more.

Until he started giving the same attention to my throat as he had my lips, I'd barely noticed the tip of his tail encircling my ankle.

"When you told me your tail was highly sensitive to a female's touch, were you talking about the end or the entire thing?" I skimmed my fingertips across his smooth blue scales, starting at the tip and not stopping until I'd reached the base.

When he tipped his head back, closed his eyes, and groaned, I smiled wickedly. "I guess that answers one of my questions."

"You have more?" Zaedon opened his eyes and wiggled his brows. "If all your questions are this pleasurable, then please continue to ask."

I should have known he'd try to turn things around to his advantage, and I wasn't going to let him. "I know you're pretty good in a fight, but how do I know you have the right kind of skills to please a ketiorra?"

Zaedon snorted. "I am an excellent fighter, but if it is proof you desire, then I will be more than happy to give you as many demonstrations as you require."

"I don't know." I absently trailed a finger along the exposed skin on his chest. "I have a lot of questions, and there are only a handful of pyteinna left. Are you sure you'll have the strength to keep up with me?"

"For you, Cara, I would starve to prove my worth."

"You may have to, but until then I wouldn't mind seeing at least one of your demonstrations." I wiggled my hips and rubbed against his erection.

He lowered his darkening turquoise gaze to my chest.

"I believe I know exactly where to start." One by one, he undid the fastenings on my shirt, then slowly peeled back the fabric until he'd exposed my breasts. He cupped one mound in his palm, brushing his thumb across the nipple before sucking it into his mouth. He took his time teasing the bud with his tongue, drawing out my whimpers until I shuddered beneath his touch.

By the time he finished with one and moved to the other, I was squirming on his lap, ready for him to take care of the steadily growing ache in the sensitive area between my legs.

"Do you have another question?"

It took me a moment to realize he'd moved his hands to my hips and was no longer proving his expertise with his tongue. So far, his skills were impressive, but the sooner he took care of the fire he'd started in other parts of my body, the happier I'd be. "Are the scales on your chest as sensitive as the ones on your tail?"

"Perhaps I should let you discover the answer for yourself." He had his shirt off in seconds, then leaned back with his hands braced on the ground.

Never one to pass up a challenge, I ran my hands over the smooth blue scales covering well-defined muscles. He sucked in a breath when I reached his abdomen, so naturally, I was encouraged to go lower.

I slipped my fingers below the waist of his pants, skimming skin and the tip of his erection.

"Cara." He wrapped his hands around my wrist to stop me. "That is not my chest."

"Fine." If the smug, arrogant male was determined to make me follow the rules I'd set, then I'd have to ask the right questions to get what I wanted. "Do your scales go all the way down the front of your legs, or do they stop at your waist?"

Zaedon chuckled. "Is that your way of saying you would like to see me naked?"

"Actually, I wanted to know what it felt like to have

your skin next to mine, but I'll understand if you have a problem with taking off your clothes."

"Why did you not say so sooner?" Mischief glinted in his gaze, and the next thing I knew, I was on my back, my boots removed, and Zaedon was pulling my pants over my ankles.

I sat up to remove my shirt, amazed by how fast he'd removed his own clothes and tossed them aside.

He sat on his haunches, making it hard not to notice his quite impressive male parts or that the scales on his chest extended to the front of his thighs. "If that particular skill meets your satisfaction, I will be happy to move on to your next inquiry."

"It does, and you can."

"You are so beautiful." He caressed my ankles, then ran his hands along my legs, spreading them as he inched higher. By the time he reached my hips, heat surged through my entire body. He seemed to have an uncanny way of knowing what I needed. He leaned forward, pressing kisses along my abdomen at the same time he teased my opening, then gently slipped his finger inside me.

"Zaedon, please." I moaned, arching my back and pushing against his hand, needing more than what he was giving me.

"Was there a question, vrincorra?" He pulled out his finger, then entered me again with two.

I could barely think, let alone devise another question, yet I knew he would continue to torture me if I didn't give him what he wanted. "I...yes. How do I know you are skilled with your shaft unless you're willing to show me?" As far as questions went, it sounded okay and was the best I could do under the circumstances.

"Another demonstration, then?" His smoldering gaze held mine.

"Yes," I murmured.

He removed his fingers, settling his hips between my

legs, the tip of his erection pressed against my opening. He wrapped his tail around my ankle, then pushed into me hard and deep. I moaned, digging my nails in his back, reveling in the feel of finally having him inside me.

The pace of his thrusts started out slow, then built in speed the closer I got to my release. He understood my body, knew what I needed. As soon as he changed the angle of his thrust, hit the spot that gave me the most pleasure, an orgasm like I'd never experienced before rippled through me.

After several hard pushes, Zaedon reached his own climax. He took a moment to catch his breath, then rolled onto his side, taking me with him. With a smile, he brushed the curls off my face. "Any more questions?"

"Nothing comes to mind at the moment." I snuggled closer.

"Should that change…"

"You will be the first to know," I said.

"Good." He wrapped his tail around the backs of my legs and closed his eyes.

Ever since I'd learned about Doyle's bounty, getting a stress-free night of sleep had been difficult. Being curled up next to Zaedon was the safest and most relaxed I'd felt in a long time. With the sound of rainfall beating steadily outside, I closed my eyes and drifted off to sleep.

# CHAPTER TWELVE

*Cara*

Even on the hard ground, a night spent entangled with Zaedon's body had been wonderful. I had no interest in leaving his arms, until I thought I heard someone outside, and jolted fully awake.

"They have to be around here somewhere." It was definitely Laria's voice, and judging by the clarity, she wasn't far from the cave's entrance.

"Zaedon, wake up," I whispered, then patted his chest when he wouldn't budge.

"Do you have more questions?" His tail snaked across the back of my legs, and he tightened his grip around my waist. "Or perhaps your lips require more testing."

I tried wiggling out of his grasp. "No, *we* need to get up and get dressed because our friends are outside."

Zaedon's eyes flew open, and he stared at the cave's narrow opening. "Which friends?"

"Found 'em." Sloane squatted on the ledge outside the entrance, beaming with a mischievous grin that added dimples to her rounded cheeks. "Hey, guys."

"Those friends," I said with a forced smile.

"Sloane, I do not think it is a good idea to intrude." Jardun's deep voice sounded close, and, though I couldn't see him, he had to be standing nearby.

"Remember our discussion about boundaries," Laria added without coming into view.

Sloane dismissed Laria, who I assumed was standing on her right, with a swipe of her hand. "It's not like I'm crawling inside with them or anything." She glanced around the cave's interior. "Though it is pretty cozy in here. Not at all what I imagined when Ellie said you might be sleeping near the fields."

"So, why are you guys here?" I had a feeling the visit didn't have anything to do with being social.

"Why don't you get dressed first, then we can talk," Laria answered.

"We'll be out just as soon as *someone* gives us some privacy." I glared at Sloane, who hadn't moved or taken the hint, because she was too busy leering at Zaedon. Not that I could blame her for staring. Zaedon was quite the sight without a shirt covering his chest. But he was my male, and I wasn't into sharing visuals with my friends, even if his male parts were covered by the blanket.

"*Sloane,*" Laria insisted when she didn't move.

"All right, geez." She got to her feet and moved away from the opening. "Laria, did you know that Zaedon's kind of hot when he's not wearing a shirt?"

I was pretty sure the growl I heard came from Jardun.

"Really?" Laria scolded. "You know Cara can hear you, right?"

"Why should she care? I'm sure she has firsthand knowledge of what he looks like naked if she spent the night with him," Sloane said offhandedly.

Even from inside the cave, I could hear Laria's exasperated sigh. "Let's go before Cara decides to strangle you with your braid and I offer to help her."

After a minute or so of silence, Zaedon pulled me into his arms. "I had hoped to keep you to myself a little longer." He caressed the back of my thigh with his tail. "Perhaps enjoy further exploration of your beautiful body."

Laria poked her head into the cave's opening, her honey-blonde braid sliding off her shoulder. "Explore later. We need to get going."

It was my turn to groan, and if I could have reached something to throw, I would have. "Laria, I swear you're worse than Sloane."

"Hey, I heard that." Sloane's teasing voice filtered in from outside.

Laria disappeared, and a few seconds later, I heard my friend's giggles fading, assuring me that they'd really started their descent down the boulders this time.

With thoughts of causing my closest friends bodily harm playing through my mind, I removed my half of the blanket and reached for my clothes.

Jardun was the leader of the vryndarr, and Khyron rarely went anywhere without him. It had to be something serious if he was here without the drezdarr. I didn't think Zaedon would keep anything from me, but I couldn't help asking anyway. "Any idea why they're here?"

"No, but whatever the reason, we will deal with it together."

If he'd told me that a few weeks ago, I would've cringed and argued that I didn't need his help. Now, things were different, and hearing that he had no intention of leaving my side warmed me to my core.

He handed me my boots along with the dagger I'd gotten from Des. "I thought I'd lost it."

"I know you prefer to use your body as a weapon, but since you have a penchant for attracting danger, I thought you might need it in the future."

"If I recall, I'm not the only one who seems to get into trouble. Are you sure you don't want to keep it?" I asked with a smirk, then slipped the dagger into the sheath hidden inside my boot.

He replied with a grunt, then tugged on his own boots. Once I finished dressing, I swiped my hand through my hair, trying to make it look decent. I missed the longer, more manageable lengths. The shorter, rebellious curls had a tendency to go in all directions after I'd slept on them.

Zaedon smiled at what I considered a failed attempt. "The wild look suits you." He leaned forward and pressed a kiss to my forehead, wiping away all thoughts of smacking him. "Are you ready?" He'd finished stuffing the bags with our supplies and set them near the entrance.

"I guess." I bent forward to get through the opening and stepped out into the morning sun, glad the storm had passed during the night. I waited for Zaedon to join me, then started the descent along the boulders.

Jardun, Laria, and Sloane were the only ones waiting for us when we reached the bottom. With threats against his life, I didn't expect to see Khyron and knew that Celeste wouldn't go anywhere without him.

"How is Celeste adapting to her new role as the drezdarrina?" Since Celeste was Khyron's ketiorra, not only had he offered to make their joining official by giving her a human wedding, but he'd also asked her to be the female equivalent of a drezdarr, to rule by his side with a common goal of uniting the ketaurrans and the humans.

"I haven't noticed anything different about Celeste as far as the ruler thing, but since the luzardee attack, she has gotten worse than Thrayn when it comes to protecting Khyron." Laria's grin insinuated there were some stories she wanted to share, but wouldn't do it in front of the males.

I gave Sloane an inquiring glance. "What did you do with Garyck?" Since the mission to rescue Vurell from Doyle's compound in the Quaddrien, it was rare not to see the grumpy ketaurran male somewhere in Sloane's general vicinity.

"Why are you asking me? It's not like we're together or anything." The regret I heard in her voice was subtle, fleeting, and quickly masked. "Although…" Sloane didn't need to finish for the rest of us to understand, not after she showed us the jeweled metal band Garyck always wore on his arm.

Sloane never talked about her life during the war before she reconnected with Laria and Celeste. Sometime during those years, she developed an ability for acquiring things that didn't belong to her. Her talent was admirable, but I had no idea why she taunted Garyck with it by continually taking his band. Of all the vryndarr, he had to be the deadliest and least approachable, yet for some unknown reason, he tolerated Sloane's antics.

Laria pinched the bridge of her nose and had to be wondering what kind of trouble Sloane's latest exploit was going to cause.

Jardun appeared mildly amused. "I asked Garyck to stay behind with Thrayn." His gaze went from me to Zaedon's hand resting on the small of my back. "You look well, my friend. It appears your new role agrees with you."

"The transition was extremely difficult, but well worth it," Zaedon said.

I knew he was referring to me specifically, and not his job as my bodyguard. When the wide grin Zaedon gave me included a wink, I returned it with an elbow to his ribs.

"Vrincorra." He groaned and rubbed his side. "Is that any way for a ketiorra to treat her male?"

"It is if you're this ketiorra and the male has a tendency to exaggerate."

Laria leaned against Jardun, slipping her arm behind his back. "I'm glad to see they finally worked things out."

Jardun laughed. "It appears to be an ongoing process."

"If you two are through, mind telling us what you're doing here?" I asked. "I'm guessing you didn't make the trip all the way out here just to check up on us." Zaedon moved closer, returning his hand to the small of my back.

"Khyron sent us to bring you both to Aztrashar," Jardun said, the humor leaving his face.

"Not the settlement? Why, what has changed?" Zaedon's tone emulated the dread coursing through my body.

"Does it have anything to do with Doyle? Does he know where I am?" After what happened in Golyndier, I'd been worried he might discover where I was staying.

Of all my friends, Laria understood me the best and knew I be worried about my grandparents. She placed a comforting hand on my arm. "Don't worry, the last we heard, Doyle didn't know where you were, so Ellie and Isaac should be safe."

"Maybe not." I took the next few minutes to explain about Derrick and the merc he'd invited into the community.

"Well, that's not good." Sloane furrowed her brows. "Please tell me you took care of them."

I didn't have to ask for more of an explanation to understand the true meaning of her question. "Isaac and the other community leaders are handling the situation with Derrick and Mike."

"And the merc?" Jardun asked.

"The male planned to sell me into slavery," Zaedon said. "I believe he has valuable information we need and should be delivered to Burke for interrogation."

He might appear unaffected by what had happened the day before, but I could feel his hand tense through the back of my shirt.

The conversation had taken a slight detour, and I still didn't know what had prompted Khyron's request. "Did Khyron say why he wants us in the city?"

"As you are aware, Khyron left Raytan in charge of his residence before we left to find Celeste at the settlement. We received word yesterday that he had critical information regarding Doyle, but would only share it in person."

"Promising news, I hope." I was relieved to hear that my family and the residents of the farming community would be safe for the time being. I was hopeful that whatever Raytan had learned about Doyle would lead to the bounty being removed from my head. Of course, Doyle would have to stop breathing for that to happen.

"We don't know, but we should get going." Laria tipped her head in the general direction of where we'd left the mini.

"Do we have time to stop by my grandparents' place first? I need a shower and to pack some clean clothes."

"Maybe you should bring along that hat you were wearing when we found you in the wastelands." Sloane raised a brow at my wild curls.

The hat she referred to had been part of my disguise when I was pretending to be a boy. "Remind me again why I tell everyone you're my friend?"

Sloane responded with a smirk.

The camaraderie and playful banter with my friends went a long way toward relieving some of my stress and made the hike back to the transport seem short.

"Where's the mini?" I asked when the only vehicle I saw was a solarveyor.

"Josh rode out with us and drove it back to the village," Laria said as she opened the vehicle's door.

As soon as we were all inside, Jardun walked to the rear of the transport, returning with a sealed container. "Ellie instructed me to give this to Zaedon. She stated something about him being a growing boy and needing these for strength." After rolling his gaze over Zaedon as if he was checking for any change in his appearance, he handed him the container. "You do not look any different to me, so it is unclear why she would think such a thing."

Laria laughed, then sat in the chair closest to the controls. "It's a human thing." She patted the seat beside her. "Come sit down, and I'll explain it on the way."

***

*Zaedon*

"This is really good." Sloane took another bite of the piece of meat she'd snatched off a platter sitting on the counter in Ellie's kitchen. I sat at the table with Jardun, Laria, and Isaac, sipping a cup of freegea and waiting for Cara to finish preparing for the trip to Aztrashar.

If Laria and Sloane had not chased me out of Cara's room earlier, stating they needed to do some female bonding with their friend, I would have enjoyed doing some bonding of my own while we bathed and taken longer to get ready.

"Thank you," Ellie said, holding out a plate of freshly made pyteinnas to Jardun. It seemed she believed he was a growing boy as well.

"Not that I was worried, but did you have a problem with the mini?" Ellie asked, her question directed at me. "Is that why you and Cara didn't come home last night?"

"The solars were drained, weren't they?" Isaac scratched the stubble on his chin, answering for me. "Those smaller vehicles get a lot of use during the harvest. Even with good weather, they have a hard time keeping up."

Sloane waved what was left of the meat in front of her face. "I'll bet spending the night in the cave had more to do with Cara finding out she's Zaedon's ketiorra than anything else."

I coughed, nearly spitting out my most recent swallow. I had forgotten Sloane did not have a problem stating the obvious, and sometimes with great detail.

"Sloane, don't you think you should have let Cara tell her grandparents herself?" Judging by the way Laria flexed her fingers, it was a good thing she was sitting on the opposite side of the table and couldn't reach Sloane.

"Why?" Sloane reached for a pyteinna. "It's not like Ellie and Isaac hadn't already figured it out."

"Speaking of figuring it out." Cara sauntered into the

room and dropped her travel bag next to mine, which was sitting on the floor next to the building's rear exit. "Is there a reason neither of you gave me a heads-up?" The annoyed glare she gave Laria and Sloane did not possess any anger.

"Would you have believed us if we had?" Laria asked.

"Probably not." Cara sat in the chair next to me, placing her hand on my thigh.

It was the first affectionate act she'd shown in front of her friends, and the simple gesture made my tail twitch.

"I don't think any of that matters." Ellie tsked. "What's important is the two of you found each other and are together now."

Ellie appeared quite pleased, and I had a feeling the older female had been in favor of our joining from the day I arrived. I would have stated my agreement, but Cara's elbow was too close to my ribs.

Jardun put a halt to the conversation by standing. "If everyone is ready, we should go."

With several affirmative replies, the members of our group said their farewells to Ellie and Isaac, then headed for the door. I would miss spending time with Cara's grandparents, but was eager to return to my role as vryndarr. I was also anxious to learn what information Raytan had discovered about Doyle and how it would affect Cara.

Cara waited until the others were finished before pulling Ellie into a hug. "If you need anything, send word to Burke. He'll know how to find us."

Ellie nodded, then cupped Cara's cheeks after she released her. "You be careful and look out for each other."

"I will." Cara blinked away the sadness filling her eyes.

She stepped away from Cara and gave me a hug as well. "Good, because I expect to see you both for the next harvest."

"I would not miss it," I said.

Ellie turned to grab a container off the counter. "It's a

long trip, so I made these for you."

Cara smiled, rolling her eyes. "You don't need to keep bribing him."

"What bribing?" Ellie sounded appalled. "He's a growing boy and will need plenty of strength to keep up with you."

"I'm pretty sure he's done growing, but the keeping-up part is right." Cara winked at me, then grabbed her bag and rushed outside.

Ellie shook her head. "You best be getting after her."

"Thank you, Ellie... For everything." I hurried to grab my bag and race after Cara. I'd reached the end of the platform when I heard Isaac call my name. I turned to find him standing in the doorway.

"I know Cara can take care of herself." Concern deepened the wrinkles around Isaac's dark eyes as he watched his granddaughter follow after our friends. "But I'm still trusting you to look out for my baby girl."

Now that I had found my ketiorra, I hoped to spend many years with her. Keeping her safe would always be my priority. "It is a difficult task, but you have my word that I will give my life if it means saving hers."

"I know you will." He scratched the top of his head. "Ellie and I kind of like having you around, so if you could both come back in one piece, we'd really appreciate it."

During my time staying with the elderly couple, I had grown quite fond of them and looked forward to returning. "It is my utmost goal."

"Good, then you better get going." Isaac patted my shoulder. "The sooner you take care of whatever you and your friends are up to, the sooner we get to see you again."

When I reached the others, they were standing next to a group of solarveyors, including Laria's and the one they had arrived in.

"What do you mean we're not taking Trixie?" Cara grasped her bag in one hand, the other planted firmly on her hip. "I finished all the repairs, and she's running perfectly."

"I know, but some of Doyle's males might recognize her, and Jardun wants to slip into the city undetected." Laria did not seem happy about the decision either. She moved next to her transport, pushing her lower lip out in an exaggerated pout as she ran her hand along the metal exterior of her treasured possession.

"What about Khyron and the others?" I asked, taking a spot on Cara's right. "How were they planning to conceal their arrival?"

"Do you remember us telling you about Joe?" Sloane asked.

"Yes." I had never met the male, but according to Celeste, he frequently sold things at the trader's market in each of the human settlements, theirs included.

His life was ended, his vehicle stolen by another human male named Travis. The despicable male had tried to take one of the young ones in Harper's care and help a group of luzardees get past the settlement's perimeter in order to attack Khyron.

Fortunately, Trevor's plan had been unsuccessful and Burke had confiscated the vehicle.

"They used his transport," Sloane said.

"Burke gave us this one since it hardly ever leaves the settlement." Jardun walked over to the vehicle, tapped a panel next to the access door, then moved to the side so Laria could enter.

Traveling under the guise of a trader was a good plan; so was using a vehicle no one would recognize. Though it would help keep Cara safe, I wondered if utilizing the old transport had been a wise choice. The dull metal exterior was rusted in places, and even I had doubts about its endurance. "Are you sure it will make it all the way to the city?"

"Nothing fell off on our way here, if that makes you feel any better." Sloane giggled as she trailed after Laria.

"It does not," I muttered.

"On the positive side, if something breaks down, you can help me fix it," Cara said.

"How is that positive?" I could not resist pinching her backside when she hauled herself into the transport.

# CHAPTER THIRTEEN

The trip to Aztrashar went by quickly without the older transport having any problems with its engine. The tension was minimal, the conversations light and playful, with everyone avoiding any topic that involved the reason we were returning to the city. Most of the time was spent catching Zaedon and me up on things that had happened during our absence from the settlement.

"How is Rygael doing?" The last time I'd heard anything about the albino ketaurran male who'd rescued Melissa from being kidnapped by Trevor, he'd been recuperating at Harper's place.

"Oh, he went back to his cave," Laria said.

After Rygael was injured, we'd learned he'd been living in the rock formations near the perimeter of the town.

"I thought for sure he'd take Harper up on her offer to stay in one of her spare rooms. What happened there?" I took a pyteinna from the container Zaedon had on his lap. He reluctantly agreed to share with everyone after I promised to cook him one of my special batches.

"Don't know, but Harper wasn't happy about it." Laria shifted sideways in her seat. Since Jardun was driving the solarveyor, she'd taken the chair next to him.

Sloane looked up from sharpening one of her blades. "She even talked to Khyron and tried to get him to order Rygael to return."

"Really, and how did that go?" I took a bite of my flat cake.

"Khyron refused, of course," Laria said. "He told her he wouldn't force the male to live anywhere he didn't feel comfortable."

Harper might not wield weapons or fight like the rest of us, but she was a strong, determined female who didn't take no for an answer. "I'd be curious to see how long it takes before Harper does something else to get her way."

"Yeah." Sloane giggled. "Especially since her interest in Rygael is more than making sure he has a nice place to stay."

"We are almost there," Jardun announced before slowing the transport.

The mood inside the vehicle changed immediately, everyone alert and prepared for any challenge or problem we might incur.

Tension thrummed through my system, and I leaned forward to get a better view through the pane above the control panel. It was late afternoon, the sunlight slowly disappearing from the green sky, leaving portions of the city cast in heavy shadows. Jardun turned right onto a road that skirted the outside of the city instead of entering via the main access.

"Where are you going?" Laria asked.

"This way is longer but will get us closer to Khyron's place without drawing too much attention."

Most likely, Doyle's males would be somewhere inside Aztrashar and concentrating on new arrivals. It didn't mean one or two wouldn't be watching alternative routes. It was how the two males who'd followed our group from the Quaddrien had been able to ambush Celeste and me on our way to the settlement.

Zaedon sealed the container and set it aside. His

transformation into a warrior appeared with the subtle fading of his grin and a growing wariness in his dark turquoise eyes. He was so busy staring out the side panes that I wondered if he realized how securely his tail was wrapped around my lower legs.

We drove past the area used by the trader's market travelers. We received a few curious glances from the handful of humans and ketaurrans who'd shut down for the day and were returning to their vehicles. I scanned their faces, watching for any change in expression or demeanor that signaled an alternative reason for their presence, and was relieved not to find any.

When we reached a guarded entrance near the rear of Khyron's dwelling, Zaedon went outside to speak with the four males, all armed with swords and wearing the dark uniforms of the drezdarr's soldiers. The conversation took less than a minute before one of the males motioned for Jardun to drive the transport inside.

I didn't remember there being this much security the last time I was here, and wondered how much of it had to do with the additional situation Doyle's bounty had caused. A situation that was putting the lives of the people I cared about in jeopardy.

"Cara, are you all right?" I hadn't realized how tense I'd gotten, or that everyone else had exited the transport, until Zaedon crouched in front of me and cupped the side of my face.

I leaned into his hand, drawing strength from its warmth. "I'm fine."

"I do not believe you are." His tone held a note of understanding, as if he knew where my thoughts had taken me.

I was glad he didn't say anything else, didn't push for an explanation I wasn't ready to give. After pulling our bags out from under the seat, he got to his feet, slinging the straps over one shoulder, then holding out his hand. "Ready?"

"Yeah." I took his hand and let him lead me past an assortment of various-sized solarveyors. As we approached the rear entrance of the multilevel building, I took a moment to appreciate the structure and the ornate design of the terraces on the upper floor. Khyron's dwelling was a lot fancier than any of the homes in the farming communities or human settlements I'd visited. The ketaurrans might not be technologically advanced when it came to communication or weapons, but they were excellent craftsmen. I was always impressed by the dwellings they'd constructed out of sand and stone.

I was fairly certain we'd be staying here a few days, and once I found out why Khyron had summoned us and got settled into our quarters, I planned to use one of the large carved stone tubs to take a long bath. I didn't think I'd have to do much convincing to get Zaedon to join me since he hadn't been happy when Sloane and Laria kept us from sharing a shower at my grandparents' place.

Once we were inside, Zaedon and I followed the sound of Laria's and Sloane's voices and found them in the gathering room of the quarters we'd shared the last time we stayed here. Khyron and Celeste were with them, but facing away from us. Thrayn saw us enter the room and acknowledged our arrival with a nod.

"I see that Khyron does not bear any new knife wounds, so I assume all is still well between you." Zaedon set our bags off to the side as he spoke to Celeste.

"It was one time." Celeste slapped her hands on her hips as she spun around to face us. "And, if you'll recall, my blade missed him by inches."

I let go of Zaedon's hand to return Celeste's hug. My friend was an expert when it came to wielding blades. If she'd meant to hit Khyron, he'd be wearing a scar. She was a couple of inches taller than me and easily draped her arm across the back of my shoulder and smiled at Zaedon. "You're alive, so either Cara hasn't tried to kill you, or you finally told her."

Zaedon grinned. "I have truly missed your humor, zyrdena."

Laria told me that Zaedon had given Celeste the ketaurran nickname, which translated to "little princess," after she'd fussed about getting sandy mud all over her favorite pair of boots.

"And yes, she is aware she is my ketiorra." Zaedon took my hand again and pulled me closer.

Khyron walked over to Zaedon, clapped him on the shoulder, then offered me a smile. He had the same tall, muscular build as the rest of the ketaurran males, but his scales were a lighter blue than Zaedon's. "I am very happy for both of you." He shot a glance at Thrayn over my shoulder. "Now if I could find a female to keep Thrayn busy, maybe he would not have so much time to hover."

Thrayn's pale green cheeks flushed. He was the youngest of the vryndarr, had the least experience with humans, and was the easiest to embarrass.

Celeste nudged Khyron's shoulder. "Just ignore him, Thrayn. You're doing a great job."

Footsteps sounded in the outside hallway right before I heard my name. I turned and smiled at the familiar ketaurran male with pale peach scales. Vurell was the drezdarr's personal physician and usually traveled with Khyron. He wasn't the most personable of males, so I was surprised when he pulled me into a breath-stealing hug.

We'd spent some time together when he'd been kept prisoner in Doyle's compound and forced, via beatings, to work with the toxins and antidotes stored in one of the labs. The same lab I'd destroyed during our escape.

"I am glad to see you are well, and that this one"—he jutted his chin at Zaedon—"appears to be unscathed."

I made a noise between a laugh and a snort. "So far, anyway."

"Glad to see you two could make it." Logan slipped into the room behind Vurell. He was Burke's second-in-command and the only human male in the group, which was a little unusual since he usually kept his distance from ketaurrans.

He'd never said much about his life during the war, but I got the impression he'd suffered some losses and had a hard time trusting anyone. The short growth of hair on his chin, combined with his dark hair and eyes, gave him an ominous look that tended to keep people at a distance. Only my friends and I knew there was a softer side to Logan that he did his best to keep hidden.

"I'm surprised to see you here. I thought you hated the city," I said.

He grinned. "I do, but since Burke couldn't make it, you get the pleasure of having me around instead."

I understood why Burke had been asked to stay behind. He had a history with Doyle, one that began during their time on the *Starward Bounty* and had gotten him injured during his mission into the wastelands. If anyone in Doyle's crew spotted him and relayed the information to their boss before we had time to implement whatever Khyron had planned, we might lose our only chance to stop him. I, on the other hand, could be used as bait. And I would gladly do it to ensure the safety of the people I cared about.

Logan had barely made it across the room and dropped onto one of the loungers when Jardun and Garyck arrived along with a ketaurran male I'd never met. I wondered if he was the Raytan the others had mentioned on several occasions. He was armed with a sword and had the same confident demeanor as the rest of the vryndarr.

His long, charcoal hair was secured at his nape. The edge of each pale green scale running along his arms and chest was unusually outlined by a darker color in the same shade. A shade that matched the vibrant intensity of his eyes.

"Raytan," Celeste said. "These are my friends Laria, Sloane, and Cara." She pointed to each of us in turn.

Once introductions were over, and before anyone had

a chance to discuss why we were here, Garyck crossed the room to stand in front of Sloane. "Little one."

Sloane was the shortest one in the group and had to tip her head back to see his face. "Did you walk all the way over her to tell me you missed me?"

"The only thing I missed was my armband." He glared and held out his hand, the hint of a smile and the swish of his golden-scaled tail making me think he wasn't as mad as he pretended.

Sloane rolled her eyes, then reached inside the bag draped over her shoulder and pulled out his band. "If you didn't want to lose it, you shouldn't have dared me to take it before I left."

Garyck replied with his usual grunt. Unlike the rest of us, Sloane could actually interpret his meaning.

"Besides, it's not like I planned on keeping it or anything." She placed it on his forearm, gave it a gentle pat, then moved to the other side of the room next to Celeste, and leaned against a lounger.

The tension, though barely noticeable, between Garyck and Sloane was new, and I wondered what had happened in my absence. I gave Laria an inquiring glance and received a confused shrug.

Zaedon must have sensed the change in our friends as well. He gave my hip a squeeze and said, "Khyron, perhaps now would be a good time to tell us why we are here."

*****

*Zaedon*

"Zaedon's right." Khyron waved his hand around the gathering room of the quarters the females shared the last time they had stayed in the city. "Make yourselves comfortable. We have much to discuss." He took Celeste's hand and led her to a seat on the nearest lounger.

The rest of the group either found a place to sit or chose a spot to stand and lean against a wall. Garyck walked over to the entrance leading into the outer hallway and closed the double doors, then took on the role of guard by remaining next to them.

Cara did not move, seemingly uninterested in doing either, so I pulled her in front of me, slipping my arms around her middle and urging her back against my chest.

"Thanks." Cara tipped her head to the side and rewarded me with a smile.

I believed we were about to face a difficult challenge, and I struggled with the urge to wrap my tail around her legs. The status of our relationship might have changed, but it was still new, and I did not want Cara to assume I was being overprotective. Instead, I sniffed her hair, the soft curls tickling my nose, the calming effect immediate.

Once we were all settled, Khyron turned to Raytan. "Please relay the information you have gathered."

Raytan was a trusted member of our team and had been left in charge when the rest of us went with Khyron to the settlement in search of Celeste. He hadn't been happy about staying behind, but had done what he'd been assigned nonetheless. After glancing around the room, he began. "Once Khyron learned that Doyle had posted a bounty on Cara, he sent word asking me to monitor activities in the city more closely. I am sure you are all aware that since the end of the war, Doyle rarely leaves the Quaddrien. He usually sends his males to do his work for him." Raytan paced as he spoke. "Several days ago, one of my sources reported news of Doyle leaving his compound and traveling to Aztrashar."

"Are you saying he's here in the city now?" Cara asked, her voice laced with excitement. "Has someone actually seen him?"

I understood her concern. Not everything we heard was reliable, and with lives at stake, confirming the accuracy of information was paramount.

Raytan stopped moving long enough to answer Cara. "Yes, I had my doubts and personally traveled to the inner city, where the mercs are known to transact their business."

That particular area of the city was run-down, the streets not safe to travel after dark. It was also where my friends and I first met Laria, Celeste, and Sloane.

Raytan toyed with the hilt of his sword. "I was able to catch a glimpse of the male and overheard another address him by his name, but was unable to discover the purpose of his visit."

"I think I might know something about that." Cara spent the next few minutes explaining what Des had told her about Doyle and his possible involvement with whoever was behind wanting Khyron and the vryndarr dead.

"And you trust this male?" Jardun asked, his dark-green gaze sparking with interest.

"I do. I've dealt with Des many times over the years, and his information is usually accurate," Cara said.

"If what Cara has learned is true, then it is imperative we capture Doyle and keep him alive for questioning," Jardun said. "If we can find out who he is working with, then it may be possible to learn who has been plotting to end Khyron's life."

After the war, there had been rumors that Sarus was dead, but none of us had actually seen a body. Jardun was convinced the male was alive and still posed a threat to Khyron and the humans.

Laria scooted to the edge of her seat. "While you were verifying, did you get an exact location where we can find him?"

"No." Raytan's frown deepened. "There were too many males with him for me to get close, and following them would have drawn attention."

Sloane asked, "If we have a good idea where Doyle is hanging out, wouldn't it be easier to send in soldiers, and have them search all the buildings?"

"It would, but we do not know who can be trusted, or if any of them were loyal to Sarus and willing to betray Khyron," Raytan said. "We cannot risk someone relaying our plans to Doyle and providing him with an opportunity to escape."

"And you can bet after your visit to the Quaddrien, he's turned his compound into an impenetrable fortress." Logan scratched the stubble on his chin. "If he gets out of the city, we may never get another chance to capture him and find out why he's here."

"Raytan, did you happen to notice if any of the males with Doyle were armed with weapons other than swords?" Cara's body stiffened when she asked the question.

"No, why?"

"During my time at the compound, I learned that Doyle had found some of the laser blasters the human survivors believed had been destroyed in the crash," Cara said.

All the vryndarr had been required to read the data files given to Khyron's sire by the humans shortly after they arrived. We all knew the weapons were capable of killing from a distance.

"There is a good chance Doyle might have brought blasters with him, but is keeping them hidden," Cara said.

"Cara makes a good point." Sloane pushed away from the wall where she'd been standing. "Swords are no match for those weapons, and there are a lot of unarmed people living near that area who could get hurt."

"I have already considered the possibility, which is why the people in this room are the only ones who are aware of the plan"—Khyron swept his hand through his hair—"and the only ones who will be going on this mission."

Khyron, as well as the rest of the males, myself included, had to be experiencing an overwhelming need to protect the females, but knew it would do no good to insist they remain behind. Having my fears confirmed

143

about the reason we had been summoned to the city did not ease my anxiety. I tightened my grip around Cara's waist, receiving a gentle caress along the scales on my arm.

"And before any of you ask, please know that I did not bring any of the advanced weapons the females found hidden in the solarveyor confiscated from Doyle during your exit from the wastelands. Until their use is absolutely necessary, they will remain safely secured back at the settlement." Khyron glanced around the room. "I am not willing to risk the lives of innocents, so if Doyle's males are armed with lasers, it is up to us to disarm them before anyone gets hurt."

A loud rap echoed through the room. Garyck looked to Khyron for approval before opening one of the doors.

"Garyck, I was looking for Vurell." Kren, whose head barely reached Garyck's shoulders, slipped around him and walked into the room. "I need…" He glanced at everyone present and froze. His pause was brief, his surprise at seeing Cara and me quickly pushed away with several blinks of his dark yellow eyes. "Raytan did not mention he was expecting the arrival of others."

"The drezdarr's affairs are none of your business," Vurell interrupted, his voice rasping with irritation. "Have you come to inform me that someone is dying?"

Kren shook his head. "No."

"Then whatever you need is not an emergency and can wait until later." Vurell's admonishment of the younger male seemed a bit harsh, but then he was not known for being polite.

My friends and I were accustomed to Vurell's gruffness, had learned to ignore it, but Kren, who had been training and assisting him for the last year, had not.

Kren clenched his fists tightly to his thighs and spoke through gritted teeth. "Of course. I am sorry for the intrusion." He bowed his head to Khyron as he slowly backed from the room.

"Impertinent male," Vurell mumbled as soon as

Garyck closed the door behind Kren, and returned to the same spot he'd been standing before his arrival. "Khyron, please continue explaining your plan, and how you expect me to keep up with the numerous injuries the team is going to incur."

\*\*\*

*Cara*

If the odds of anyone on the team sustaining injuries hadn't been high, I would have found Vurell's sarcastic comment amusing. We were all highly skilled, and if we were going up against males with blades, my concern would be minimal. Doyle was ruthless, leaving me little doubt that he'd brought lasers with him, or that his visit was somehow tied to what I learned from Des.

"Khyron, you're not planning to stay behind, are you?" I already knew the answer. The drezdarr would never ask any of us to do what he wasn't willing to do himself.

"As if," Celeste huffed.

This mission was going to be our most dangerous yet, and we needed every advantage we could get. I pulled out of Zaedon's arms and walked across the room.

"Cara, where are you going?" Zaedon asked.

"To get this." I reached into my bag, glad I'd thought to stuff one of the stun sticks I'd taken from the bandits inside before we left. I'd already given the other one to Josh so he could study the design and try to replicate it. "Some additional protection."

"Where did you get a stun stick?" Khyron furrowed his brow, his narrow turquoise gaze going from me to Zaedon.

"It is a story for another time," Zaedon said, uncomfortably shifting his stance.

Zaedon was a proud male, and I couldn't fault him for not wanting to tell the others how he'd been zapped into unconsciousness.

"This one has been modified." I walked over to Khyron and handed it to him. "It seems the luzardee found a way to increase the voltage."

"I have heard about these, but never seen one before. May I?" Thrayn stepped around the lounger and held out his hand to Khyron.

"How does it work?" Thrayn gripped both ends as he studied the stick.

"Thrayn, no, don't touch…" My warning came too late.

He accidentally activated the control and gave himself a jolt. His arms shook, his roar filling the room. If not for Laria's quick thinking, along with a well-placed kick to the center of the stick with the heel of her boot, Thrayn might not have let go of it.

The stick hit the floor first, followed by Thrayn dropping to his knees, then falling face forward.

No one moved to help him.

"I can't believe he actually shocked himself." Laria bit her bottom lip, trying hard not to laugh.

"I can." Sloane walked over and knelt beside Thrayn, then rolled him on his back. "Looks like he's still breathing, so he must be okay."

"How long will he be out?" Jardun asked as he picked up the stick.

"Several hours, maybe more." I based my guess on the amount of time Zaedon had been out and the size similarities between Thrayn and him.

"There are days…" Khyron pinched the bridge of his nose. "It would serve him right if we just left him here until he wakes."

"We aren't going to leave him on the floor. Not unless you were planning to sleep alone until we return to the settlement."

Khryon released an outraged gasp. "Zadierra, you would not…"

"Wouldn't I?" Celeste scooted out of Khyron's reach when he tried to take her hand.

I was surprised Khyron hadn't learned that he was outmatched when it came to a battle of wills with Celeste. Or maybe he had and enjoyed the challenge.

"Fine, Zaedon and Jardun can put him in your old room since *you* will most definitely not be needing it." Khryon reached for Celeste again, his attempt to pull her into his arms successful. He probably assumed he'd won the battle, but the wink Celeste shot in my direction said otherwise.

With a giggle, Laria draped her arm over my shoulder. "See what you've been missing?"

# CHAPTER FOURTEEN

*Zaedon*

Besides apprehending Doyle, preventing injury to any of the ketaurrans and humans living near the part of the city where Raytan had seen the mercenary and his males was our top priority. After Jardun and I had ensured that Thrayn was resting comfortably in Celeste's old room, the group spent the remainder of the afternoon developing a plan.

I pitied Thrayn when he woke up and found us gone. Not only was he going to be disappointed he was left behind, but the pain from the jolt, combined with the throbbing in his head, would be less than tolerable.

Thrayn was doing well as a vryndarr, but he was young and had a lot to learn. He still tried Khyron's patience, and his latest curiosity with the stun stick would no doubt earn him months of teasing from the other males as well as the females in the group.

Nightfall came quickly, leaving me no time to spend alone with Cara or talk her out of the dangerous plan she'd suggested. A plan everyone else seemed to think was our best option. I, of course, did not agree since Cara would be taking the highest risk.

"You are all clear on what you need to do, correct?" Khyron's commanding whisper drew me from my thoughts.

Everyone in the group except me gave him an affirmative nod before pulling the hoods of their jackets over their heads.

"Zaedon?" I had voiced my objections earlier, so Khyron knew I was not happy that another male would be accompanying her.

"Clear." I reluctantly agreed.

I had learned that Cara was not the only one good with disguises. Logan was equally talented. He would pretend to be a merc, then ask to be taken to Doyle so he could hand over Cara for the bounty. The rest of us would take strategic positions and follow. Once we discovered Doyle's location, we would move in and, with any luck, apprehend him without a lot of bloodshed.

"Khyron, give us a minute." Cara took my hand and pulled me away from the group.

Once we were alone, I wrapped my arms around her waist, hopefully not for the last time. "You know you do not have to do this."

"Yes, I do." She placed her warm hands on my cheeks. "We can't spend the rest of our lives hiding and worrying about Doyle. I need to know that my grandparents will be safe, and you need to find out who is behind the attacks on Khyron."

To hear her say "We" and not "I," to hear that she now considered me to be a part of her future, helped ease some of my trepidation. I pressed my forehead to hers. "I know, but it does not make it any easier for me to agree with your plan."

"I'm not thrilled about it either, but it's the only way, and we both know it."

\*\*\*

*Cara*

Logan and I walked along a darkened back street, the only light available coming from several glow emitters attached to the exterior walls on a couple of the dwellings. We stopped a block away and around the corner from a run-down building that housed a bar and an upper floor with rooms used by visitors. The walkway outside was the last place Raytan had seen Doyle.

He fastened a binding around my wrists. "You ready to do this?"

He'd done a good job hiding his identity. Even I hadn't recognized him when he'd first joined our group earlier. I had no idea where he'd gotten the eye patch or what he'd used on his face to make him seem more intimidating. When this mission was over, I planned to ask him.

"Yeah, just make sure you do whatever it takes to make this look authentic. No holding back." Mercs didn't have a problem with abusing their prisoners. I could deal with some pain and bruising if it meant stopping Doyle. Zaedon wouldn't be so understanding, which was why I'd waited until Logan and I were alone to say anything.

"When have you ever known me to hold back?"

"Good point." I twisted my wrists, testing the binding to make sure I wouldn't have any trouble escaping later. Since I had a reputation for using my hands instead of blades to fight, Doyle could decide to switch to shackles. As a backup, I brought along the thin dagger I'd purchased from Des. Hopefully, if Doyle's males decided to check me for weapons, they wouldn't think to search my boots.

"Shall we?" I raised my arm for him to grab.

Being convincing also required a little acting on my part, so when he dragged me toward the building, I pretended to struggle.

As soon as we got close to the building, two males stepped out of the shadows, one I recognized, the other I didn't. If I knew Doyle, there were more males posted close by who wouldn't make their presence known until it was necessary.

Gordon was slimmer and shorter than the beefier male standing next to him. I hadn't interacted with him much when I stayed at the compound, but I knew he'd been friends with Rick and Neil, the males who'd ambushed Celeste and me on our way to the settlement about a month ago. He wasn't going to be happy if he ever found out the males were dead and that Logan and I had been partly responsible for their deaths.

"Stop right there." Gordon fingered the hilt of his sword. "This area is off-limits, so unless you want trouble, you need to turn around and head back the way you came."

"Rumor has it Doyle's in the city, and I'm here to collect my reward," Logan said.

Gordon's dark gaze flickered with suspicion. "You got a name?"

"You can call me Roy." The lie flowed easily from Logan's lips.

"Well, Roy, Doyle doesn't see anybody, not without an invitation."

I wondered if Gordon realized he'd slipped up and confirmed his boss's location.

Logan tipped his head in my direction. "He will when he finds out what I brought him."

"You don't mind if we have a look first, do you?" the other male asked.

"Be my guest," Logan said.

Letting Gordon get close to me was a risk, but as long as he didn't try to hurt me or unsheathed his sword, Logan wouldn't use the blade he had hidden inside his long jacket.

Logan's compliance didn't seem to put either of the males at ease. While Gordon moved toward me, his friend warily watched the walkway behind us.

Gordon grabbed the back of my hood and wasn't gentle when he yanked it off my head, pulling some of my hair in the process. "Well, I'll be damned if it isn't Cara, or would you prefer we still call you Carl?"

Carl was the name I'd used when I passed myself off as a boy during my stay at the compound. I glared at Gordon, refusing to show any fear. "Either works fine for me."

"Enjoy the attitude and smart mouth while you can, 'cause it won't last long once Doyle gets ahold of you," the other male said with a snicker.

"Let's go." Gordon turned to head toward the building.

"I think we'll wait for Doyle out here." Logan grabbed my arm again, signaling me to stay where I was.

We had no idea how many males we'd be dealing with inside. Things would go a lot easier, with fewer casualties, if we could lure him outside.

"I'm afraid it doesn't work that way. If you want to get paid, you follow us inside." Gordon held up his hand, and four other males appeared in the walkway. "Otherwise, we take the female anyway, and you get nothing."

Logan's bluff had been worth a try. On the upside, we now knew how many males were standing guard. If Zaedon and the others stuck to the plan, they'd be close enough to hear our conversation. Once we entered the building, they'd incapacitate the other males, then come in after us.

Logan shrugged off the newcomers with a snort. "Guess we'll be going inside."

"Smart choice." Gordon took the lead while the other male waited for us to follow, then brought up the rear.

The inside of the bar was no different from the others I'd visited. The wooden walls were bare, decor not an important commodity. Round tables were scattered across the room on my right, several of them occupied by a handful of human males and a couple of females. Judging by their clothes, their cautious stares, and the blades strapped to their hips, they were all mercs. Whether or not they worked for Doyle or someone else, I had no way of knowing.

The only ketaurrans in the room were the male behind the bar and a young female, possibly in her late twenties, who was serving drinks. Both had earthy sienna-colored scales and dark hair with red highlights, the female's a more vibrant shade of crimson. They had similar facial features, making it apparent they were related, with the male a year or so older than her.

We were halfway across the room, headed for a corridor in the back, when the female squealed. One of the male patrons had grabbed her around the waist with her arms pinned against her sides, and was pulling her onto his lap. The male sitting across from him laughed and leered, ready to join in on whatever fun the first one had planned for her. Even Gordon and the other male had stopped to watch what was happening.

It might ruin all our plans, but there was no way I was going to stand by and let the males do whatever they wanted to her. Logan must have felt the same way. His grip on my arm tightened, and the muscles along his jaw twitched.

Thankfully, neither of us had to do anything, because the male preparing drinks beat us to it.

His enraged snarl echoed through the room. "Let. Her. Go." He enunciated each word, following up his ominous threat by pulling out a short blade and aiming it at the male accosting the female.

The male quickly released her, keeping his hands in the air until she'd reached the bar. "Sorry, Vaden. I was just having a little fun."

Vaden kept his dark green eyes leveled at the male and tapped the blade against his palm. "Touch my sister again, and you will not have any parts left to have *fun* with."

After a few laughs and guffaws, the patrons returned to their conversations and drinking, acting as if nothing had happened.

Vaden walked around the bar, still gripping the blade, and placed a comforting hand on the female's shoulder. "Cianna, are you all right?"

"Fine, but..." Cianna glanced at the binding on my wrists, probably assuming the worst, then gave Vaden what appeared to be a silent plea for him to intercede on my behalf.

If Vaden was like the other ketaurran males I knew, he'd be honor-bound to help me because I was a female. The last thing Logan and I needed was for Vaden and his sister to get involved. It could cost them their lives and ruin our plans to get Doyle. When his gaze locked with mine, I shook my head, hoping he understood.

Several seconds passed before he finally acknowledged my request with a brief nod. "It is none of our concern," he said to his sister, then returned to manning the bar.

Gordon had also been paying attention to the sibling's conversation. "This way," he said once he realized Vaden wasn't going to cause him any problems.

After taking a shorter corridor that branched off the main hallway, he stopped in front of a door, then briefly pressed his ear against the wood to listen before knocking.

"What?" The bellow from inside the room belonged to Doyle, reminding me that he was a bad combination of unpredictable and ruthless, neither of which I looked forward to dealing with.

"It's Gordon and Paul, and we've got a surprise for you."

The door flew open. "I hate sur..." Doyle's glare landed on me, and his lips curled into a malicious grin, making it hard not to cringe.

The left side of his face now had two long scars resembling claw marks running from his cheekbone to his jaw. They were more than likely the result of his encounter with the snakkrils that attacked his solarveyor during our escape from the Quaddrien.

It was too bad the snakelike creature hadn't sunk its poison-laced fangs into his flesh. It would have made life a whole lot easier for my friends and me, not to mention anyone else he decided to terrorize.

"Cara, you're one surprise I don't mind getting." Doyle stepped out of the way.

When I didn't move, Gordon shoved me into the room, leaving Logan and Paul standing near the doorway.

The room was a little larger than I'd expected. To the right was an unmade bed, the blankets tossed haphazardly across the middle. A ketaurran male sat at a table adjacent to a shuttered windowpane on the left. Pale orange scales spread across the portion of his broad chest not covered by his vest. Seemingly annoyed by our intrusion, he tapped the side of a mug that was partially filled with a golden liquid.

Whatever we'd interrupted must have been important. When I continued to stare, he quickly adjusted the edge of his long coat to cover his hip, but not before I got a glimpse of what looked like a laser blaster.

He glared at me with dark amber eyes the entire time it took him to down the last of his drink and get to his feet. "Doyle, I will be leaving now."

Doyle snapped his head toward the male. "You don't need to go. You might even enjoy what comes next."

"I am not interested in your plans for this female. Contact me tomorrow. We can finish our business then." The male dismissed Doyle by heading for the door and not bothering to give him another glance.

When he walked past Logan, his gaze lingered longer than necessary. I expected him to say something to Doyle that might expose us. Once he left the room and closed the door without saying another word, I released the breath I'd been holding.

For whatever reason, Doyle hadn't noticed Logan and

wasn't paying any attention to Gordon or Paul. I took a few steps farther into the room, hoping to keep it that way.

"There's a penalty for people who cross me, Cara. Not only did you spy on me, but you destroyed my lab and stole from me." Doyle leaned forward, inches from my face, lips curled into a threatening sneer. "I want my property back."

I fought the urge not to back away. "Sorry, but I have no idea what you're talking about." Antagonizing him was never a smart thing, but with him standing this close, it gave me the opportunity to slip the rope off one wrist without drawing attention.

My mind anticipated the pain that was coming a second before his hand connected with my cheek. It was a good thing he hadn't used his fist; otherwise, I'd be on my knees, and the painful sting radiating along my jaw would hurt a lot worse.

"The weapons, Cara. Where are they?" He raised his hand, fingers curled into a tight fist.

I was ready for the punch, would use it to my advantage to disable him. Out of my periphery, I could see Logan inching toward Gordon and Paul. I knew the minute I grabbed Doyle that Logan would keep them away from me and work on disarming them.

Doyle and I continued to glare at each other. The instant he'd changed his mind, the angry flicker disappeared from his dark eyes.

"I have a better idea." Doyle lowered his arm. "My males and I haven't had a female to pass around in quite a while. By the time we're finished with you, you'll tell me what I want to know."

The thought of Doyle touching me was revolting enough, but the chuckle I heard from the other males made me nauseous.

"Hell, you'll probably even beg me to kill you." Doyle undid his belt and placed it, along with his sword, on the table.

I had a sarcastic remark on the tip of my tongue, but Logan picked that moment to make his presence known.

"Hey," Logan snapped. "The female belongs to me, and until I get paid, no one is laying a finger on her."

# CHAPTER FIFTEEN

*Zaedon*

Khyron had us split up into teams. Celeste and Raytan would accompany him. Laria went with Jardun, leaving Garyck and Sloane to work with me. Vurell was not a warrior, but refused to be left behind. Rather than increase the odds of encountering more mercs if we tried to get Doyle through Aztrashar on foot, Vurell became our decoy. It was his job to take a solarveyor, drive around the perimeter until he was certain no one was following him, then meet us at a designated location for extraction.

All the vryndarr were trained to be experts at stealth and staying hidden. The dark colors we wore helped us blend into our surroundings. Even Laria, Celeste, and Sloane were adept at not being seen.

I had chosen a location where I could remain in the shadows and not lose sight of Cara. I had to keep telling myself that Logan and Cara knew what they were doing, that every time I saw the male roughly jerk her around it was part of the roles they played. That I should not entertain thoughts of hurting the male later.

Cara had good judgment. She had known Logan a lot

longer than me, trusted him with her life, and expected me to do the same. It was difficult to wait in the darkness and listen to their conversation with Doyle's males. Even more difficult when one of them ripped the hood from Cara's head and she flinched to hide the pain it caused.

"Zaedon, we're back." Sloane announced her and Garyck's return with a whisper.

They went to check out the perimeter of the adjoining building and had been gone less than five minutes.

"What did we miss?" she asked.

"It appears Logan's attempt to lure Doyle outside has failed." I motioned toward the additional males who had appeared from various locations along the walkway.

"Yeah, but now we know how many males he had watching the building," Sloane said.

It did not matter that Logan was going with Cara, I was not happy about her entering the building, and Sloane's attempt to be positive did little to alter my feelings.

"Draeck, there are more mercs inside." From my vantage point, I'd gotten a partial glimpse of the bar's interior.

Garyck must have seen them too, because he placed his hand on my shoulder. "We will not let anything happen to your ketiorra."

As soon as the door closed behind the male following Logan, Garyck motioned for Sloane and me to follow him toward the narrow walkway that led to the back of the building.

"Where are we going?" Sloane kept her voice low as she raced to keep up with our longer strides. "I thought we were supposed to help the others take out the guards."

"Our help is not necessary," Garyck said, then stopped to peer at the rear of the building.

When Sloane wrinkled her nose in confusion, I explained, "There are more males inside, which will make it difficult for Logan and Cara to get Doyle out without being seen." Most structures in the city had a back entrance. If one was not available, we would find another way to enter.

With only two small glow emitters attached to the exterior wall, the area surrounding the walkway was cast in shadows. "One male guards the entrance." Garyck pointed toward the human leaning against the building. His average height and build posed no threat. Other than the blade on his hip, he did not appear heavily armed.

"I've got this." She squeezed past Garyck and me.

He snarled when she dodged his grasp and moved toward the center of the walkway. "Little one, do not…"

She winked, ignoring his command, and kept walking. I knew all too well what frustrating thoughts Garyck was currently entertaining. I had experienced similar emotions when Cara had engaged the two male bandits.

Garyck never openly discussed his feelings, yet by his actions, I suspected Sloane might be his ketiorra. It was unclear why he had not attempted to claim her, but unless he wanted to talk about what was going on with the female, I would not ask.

To interfere now might get Sloane harmed or cause the male to alert the others. All we could do was wait and let her execute her plan.

Sloane sauntered closer to the male. "Hey, there."

"Sweetheart, you shouldn't be back here." The male pushed away from the wall, his gaze traveling along her body, then returning to her face.

"I guess I got lost." She stopped in front of him, turning so we could see her profile. "I don't suppose you know where I could get a drink?"

"There's a bar around front." He ran a finger along her arm. "But I wouldn't be opposed to you staying so we could get to know each other better."

"Really?" Sloane eased closer, then placed her hands on his shoulders.

"Oh yeah." The male gripped her hips, his dark gaze dropping to her breasts.

Garyck growled, and I grabbed his arm, hoping I would not have to restrain him.

Sloane's next move saved me the trouble. "Sorry, that's never going to happen. You're just not my type." She brought her knee up fast and hard, then took several steps back. I might approve of Sloane's method, but hearing the male's pain-filled grunt made my tail twitch. When he grabbed his crotch and dropped to the ground, I glimpsed a hint of admiration in Garyck's amber gaze.

Rushing to assist Sloane was not necessary. The next blow with her knee caught the side of the male's head, knocking him into the building and rendering him unconscious.

By the time we reached her, she was squatting next to him and removing the knife from his belt.

She answered Garyck's inquiring frown. "There's no such thing as having too many blades." She grinned as she got to her feet, then tucked the sheath into the back of her pants. "Shall we?"

She made it two steps before her attempt to reach the rear entrance was blocked by Garyck, who seemed determined to keep her from going first.

"Seriously?" She groaned, then waited for him to enter.

The door opened into an empty hallway. I heard the low rumble of voices mixed with occasional laughter coming from the bar on the left. There were two closed doors across from us and one at the end of the corridor on the right. There was also a staircase off to one side that lead to the upper level.

There was no sign of Cara and Logan, and Doyle's room could be anywhere in the building. The longer it took us to find it, the more agitated I became.

"Where do we start looking?" Sloane appeared confident, but I heard the concern in her voice.

"We need to split up. Garyck and you can take the upper level, and I will search the rooms down here." I said, reaching for my blade.

I waited from them to reach the stairs, then silently crept across the hall to the first room. The door was unlocked, making it easy to slip inside. I was greeted by darkness and did not need to activate an emitter to know the room was empty.

There was always a chance someone from the bar might venture along the corridor, so I held the door open a crack and peered outside. Confident I was still alone, I made my way to the next room. I gripped the handle, ready to enter, when I heard footsteps behind me.

"What do you think you are doing?" A female's voice scolded me as if I were a young one.

I slowly turned to find a young ketaurran female with reddish-brown scales. She glared at me with fierce amber eyes and clutched a tray in front of her as if it were a deadly weapon she would have no problem smacking me with.

"I am searching for a female," I said.

She misunderstood my intent and huffed. "We do not provide that service here."

"This female is human, would have been brought in as a prisoner." I dropped my hands to my sides, hoping I would appear less intimidating. "I mean her no harm. I only want to help," I added when she continued to scrutinize my intent.

"Then go quickly." Her gaze jumped toward the door at the end of the hall, then back to me. "The male who stays in that room is dangerous. Far worse than any of the others."

No sooner had she turned and hurried back toward the bar than a loud thud and what sounded like wood shattering erupted from inside the room.

With my heart threatening to explode from my chest, I tightened the grip on my knife and headed for the door.

***

*Cara*

"Who are you?" Doyle glared at Logan as if seeing him for the first time, his eyes getting bigger. "Wait, I know you. You worked on Burke's security team onboard the *Starward Bounty*."

As far as I knew, Logan hadn't interacted with Doyle since leaving the ship, but even with his disguise, we knew there was a risk he might be recognized. Logan must have figured there was no point in denying the truth, because he pulled off the eye patch and shoved it in his pocket.

Now that his identity had been discovered, the only thing that mattered was getting Doyle out of here and finding the rest of the team without either of us getting hurt.

"You idiots," Doyle snapped at Gordon and Paul. "Did you bother to find out who he was before you brought him in here?"

"Well, kind of," Gordon stammered. "He said his name was Roy, and I knew how badly you wanted the female, so I..." He glanced at Paul looking for support, but the male was smart enough not to say anything.

Logan always told my friends and me that if we knew a fight was inevitable, it was better to be the first one to attack than to be the one on the receiving end. Following his own advice, Logan didn't give Paul a chance to draw his sword. He doubled his fist and punched him in the gut, followed by a blow to the jaw.

Logan was a big guy who worked out a lot, and I knew from experience how hard he could hit. Paul wasn't prepared for Logan's fast moves and ended up falling backward and toppling over the corner of the bed, then landing on the floor. I knew Paul wasn't getting up any time soon, and so did Logan.

"You should have checked us for weapons too." Logan smirked, then pulled out the small knife he had hidden inside his jacket.

Doyle had a bad temper and didn't like being outsmarted. Judging by the red spreading along his throat and cheeks, Logan's comment hadn't helped. "Take care of him," he snapped at Gordon, then turned to grab his sword.

I was closer and snatched it first, then spun to keep it out of his reach. I was never a fan of the longer blades and would have thrown it in a corner if I didn't think Doyle or one of the other males would go after it.

Logan was fighting with Gordon, his small knife no match for the other male's larger blade. "Logan, heads up," I called, then tossed the sword in his direction. As soon as I released the blade, Doyle slammed me into the wall. He wrapped his hands around my throat and squeezed.

Normally, most people would react to being choked by clawing at the hands cutting off their air supply. I'd been trained to think differently, to retaliate by going after a sensitive area that would ensure my release.

I grabbed a handful of Doyle's hair and yanked. At the same time, I worked my other hand between us, grabbing his male parts and twisting as hard as I could.

Doyle snarled and wrenched away from me. "You bitch. I'm going to kill you for that."

I would have made a sarcastic comment, but I was too busy rubbing my sore throat and gasping in air.

A few seconds later, Gordon hit the ground and wouldn't be getting back up, not with Logan's small knife sticking out of his chest.

Now that Doyle's males were incapacitated and it didn't look like anyone else was coming to help him, he must have realized fighting Logan and me was futile. He picked up a chair and used it to smash through the wooden shutter and the windowpane behind it. He dove through the opening, muttering a curse when he landed, then disappearing into the darkness.

We'd gone through too much, and I wasn't about to let him get away. I turned to go after Doyle, and hadn't noticed that Paul had regained consciousness until I saw him swiping at me with his sword.

"Cara, look out!" Logan yelled as he shoved me out of the way.

It was a good thing I had my arm raised; otherwise, I would have hit my head when I collided with the wall. I turned to find Logan clutching his chest. When he'd pushed me aside, he hadn't moved fast enough to keep the blade from slicing through his sleeve and cutting across his forearm and part of his shoulder.

"This one's for Gordon." Paul swiped at Logan, the room filling with the sound of metal clashing.

The longer the males fought, the more blood soaked the patch on the fabric surrounding Logan's injury. His defensive moves weakened with each swing of Paul's sword. I didn't enjoy taking a life, but at this rate, if I didn't do something, Paul would overpower Logan.

Moving slowly so Paul wouldn't notice, I retrieved the dagger I'd gotten from Des from inside my boot. I couldn't afford to miss and patiently waited for an opening. Paul backed Logan into a corner, and when he raised his sword to deliver a damaging blow, I threw the dagger.

The blade pierced Paul's back between his shoulders. He shrieked and dropped his sword, trying desperately to dislodge it. With an upward stroke, Logan drove his blade into Paul's midsection, finishing what I had started.

"Draeck, Logan. What were you thinking?" I helped him around Paul's body and urged him to take a seat on the edge of the bed.

Logan grabbed the end of a blanket and pressed it against the wound to stop the bleeding. "I was thinking about what Zaedon was going to do to me if I broke my promise and let something bad happen to you." He winced when he tried to laugh.

"Yeah, he…" I didn't get a chance to finish. The door opened behind me, and I spun around, expecting to see more of Doyle's males.

\*\*\*

*Zaedon*

Finding Cara standing next to a dead human male's body, poised to attack, was not what I expected when I heard the loud thud and rushed to open the door at the end of the corridor. I was not surprised by the room's condition. Chairs were tossed on their sides, the only pane shattered, leaving a gaping hole. The wooden shutter was cracked and splintered in several places.

"Zaedon." She straightened, her dark eyes sparkling with relief and happiness. "You missed all the fun." She stepped over the body and into my welcoming arms.

"It would seem you are correct." I grinned, then pulled her closer, needing to feel her warm body against mine. I sniffed her neck, letting her scent calm me.

"I hate to interrupt your reunion, but someone needs to go after Doyle, and I'd really like to get out of here and find a medical kit before I bleed to death." Logan's annoyed voice was laced with humor.

I had been too busy easing my worry over Cara, I had not noticed Logan or that he'd been injured. He had a blanket pressed to his shoulder and his face had lost some of its color.

As much as I wanted to continue holding her, it wasn't safe to linger, not with so many mercs occupying the bar. I released Cara and moved to help her with Logan.

Sloane appeared in the doorway, wrinkling her nose at the males on the floor. "Looks like you guys have been busy."

"Where's Garyck?" Cara asked. "Wasn't he supposed to be with you guys?"

"Oh, he's helping the others clean up the bar. If you know what I mean." Sloane hitched her thumb over her shoulder, wiggled her brows, then noticed Logan and frowned. "What happened to you?"

"Logan tried to play hero and jumped in front of a blade that was meant for me." Cara held out her hand for Logan to give her the bloodied blanket, then tossed it on the bed.

"What?" The dread I had experienced earlier was not unwarranted.

"Don't give me one of your smug looks, and the words 'I told you so' better not leave your lips," Cara warned.

I was certain Cara and I would be having a more in-depth discussion about what happened later. Logan, however, had risked his life to keep my ketiorra safe and earned a lifetime of respect. "Logan, I am glad you are a male of your word, and very grateful for your sacrifice."

"I'd say anytime, but this draecking hurts, so if we could..." He tipped his head toward the open doorway.

"Of course." I draped his arm over my shoulder and helped him into the corridor.

When we entered the bar, Celeste was sitting on the long counter, swinging her legs and balancing a half-filled mug on her lap. The female who had told me where to find Cara was standing behind the bar filling several more mugs with ale.

Cara glanced at the empty tables and chairs. "What did you do with all the bodies?"

"No bodies." Celeste took a sip of her drink. "Laria and Jardun went after the two mercs that escaped. The rest are in the back. Vaden, the bar's owner, is letting Khyron use one of his storage rooms until he can get some soldiers here to take them back to the palace for questioning."

Though I did not fully understand the reference,

Celeste and her friends had been referring to Khyron's home as a palace ever since the first night they stayed there.

The female smiled at me, then Cara. "I am glad you are all right and that he found you in time."

"Found me?" Cara gazed at me curiously.

"The female caught me searching rooms and pointed me in the correct direction," I said.

The female pursed her lips. "I prefer to be called Cianna rather than female."

"Of course." I grinned at the spirited female and bowed my head. "Cianna."

She smiled her approval, then pushed the filled mugs across the counter. "Please help yourselves."

"Thanks." Sloane took one of the glasses and joined Celeste at the bar.

Cara pulled out a chair for Logan. "Cianna, do you have a medical kit?"

"Why?" Her amber gaze went to Logan, and she gasped. "Oh yes." She reached underneath the bar, then hurried around the counter, carrying a small container.

"Cianna, what are you doing?" A ketaurran male with the same reddish-brown scales and similar features walked into the room, with Khyron, Raytan, and Garyck following behind him.

"The male is hurt, and I am seeing to his injuries." Cianna clutched the kit to her chest.

"I am certain his friends will take care of him," Vaden said.

Cianna slapped one hand on her hip, her tail swishing rapidly. "You will stop being an overbearing sibling and let me help him, or I will pull off your scales like I did when we were younglings."

Vaden did not appear to be a male who intimidated easily, yet he placed his hand protectively over his chest.

Cianna turned her back on her brother, then knelt in front of Logan and placed the kit on the floor.

"Come on, Vaden." Khyron clapped him on the shoulder. "Why don't you join us for a drink and let Cianna take care of Logan?"

Vaden continued to frown at his sister, but walked over to the bar and stood next to Raytan. Garyck picked up a mug and moved to stand on the opposite side not far from Sloane.

"I guess we don't need to worry about Logan anymore." Cara held out her hand and pulled me toward the bar.

I glanced over my shoulder, amused to see Logan watching Cianna with great interest. "It appears not."

After several swallows of the bitter ale Cianna had poured for us, the door leading to the walkway outside opened. Laria entered first, with Jardun following close behind her.

"So, did you find them?" Celeste asked Laria.

"No." Laria walked over to the counter and picked up two mugs, then handed one to Jardun. "We stopped looking after we found Doyle."

"Seriously, you found him?" Cara was about to take a drink and lowered her mug.

"Then where is he?" Sloane sounded skeptical.

"In a walkway behind a building not far from here." Jardun spoke directly to Khyron. "Someone slit his throat."

Though cutting the evil male's throat had been something I had wanted to do myself, the news was unsettling. With Doyle gone, Cara and her family would be safe, but without the information we hoped the male would provide, we were no closer to discovering the identity of those who had poisoned Khyron and were still trying to take his life.

"Maybe it was the ketaurran male I saw in Doyle's room when we first arrived," Cara said.

"What male?" I asked. "Other than the human males guarding the building, I did not see anyone leave after you

169

arrived."

"Us either," Celeste said.

"Do you think he's still in the building?" Laria glanced at the hallway behind us.

"No, Garyck and I checked all the rooms on the upper level." Sloane set her empty mug on the counter.

"Then he must have gone out the back before Sloane disarmed the guard," I said.

"Maybe he's the one responsible for killing Doyle. I could have sworn he had a laser blaster tucked under his jacket. He told Doyle they could finish their business in the morning, but didn't mention any details." Cara tapped her nails on the bar. "He also seemed really interested in Logan. I thought for sure the two of them knew each other."

"There was something familiar about him," Logan said. "But I don't remember ever meeting him."

The right half of Logan's chest was bare, and Cianna applied a sealant over the cleaned wound.

Raytan turned to Khyron. "It sounds like finding the male might provide us with the answers we are searching for."

"I agree," Khyron said. "It is something we can discuss in the morning. For now, I think we should return to the solarveyor before Vurell decides we have been gone too long and comes looking for us."

Khyron helped Celeste off the bar, then turned to Vaden. "I do not believe it is safe for Cianna and you to stay here and think you should consider spending the next few days in my dwelling. It will also give my males time to remove the bodies and repair any damage we caused."

It was a well-known fact that any suggestion made by the drezdarr was not a request but a polite order that required compliance. It was evident by Vaden's concerned expression that he did not want to leave his home and was contemplating the ramifications of refusing.

Cianna, on the other hand, seemed excited by the

invitation. I wondered how much of her enthusiastic smile had to do with staying in the drezdarr's home or being able to see more of Logan.

"Vaden," Cianna insisted.

Vaden released the heavy sigh of a male who knew he was not going to win. "Thank you, Khyron. My sister and I would be honored to stay at your dwelling."

# CHAPTER SIXTEEN

*Zaedon*

It had been several days since our team had gone after Doyle. Our efforts to find the ketaurran male who Cara had seen in Doyle's room had failed. If he was still in Aztrashar, which was doubtful, he had found a good place to hide.

My nights were spent pleasing my ketiorra, the early mornings spent with her wrapped in my arms. Today was the first time since I had claimed her that I woke from a sleepy haze to find the spot next to me empty.

I braced my upper body on my elbows to get a better look around the room, hoping I would find her close by. When I did not see her, I grumbled and reached for the blanket covering my lower half. I had one foot off the bed when Cara appeared in the doorway leading into the gathering room.

The quarters I shared with the other vryndarr were similar to the one Cara had previously shared with her friends. Individual sleeping rooms positioned around a main area filled with several loungers, and connected with a hallway that led to other parts of the building.

"Bad mood?" Cara asked as she leaned against the doorframe.

Her feet were bare, the only thing covering her body her pants and my oversized vest. She had not bothered to tame her curls, their wild state both cute and enticing.

I continued to sit up, dropping my other leg over the edge of the bed. "I did not enjoy waking up to find you missing." I did not care that I sounded like a spoiled young one. I had waited a long time to find my ketiorra, and now that I had her, I was selfish about the time I got to spend with her.

"I had a couple of things I needed to take care of and didn't want to wake you." She padded toward me.

I got to my feet and reached for her hips, my shaft hardening at the prospect of dragging her back into bed and having her pressed against my naked body. "What was this important task?"

She slipped her hands over my shoulders. "I convinced Khyron to let us spend the next two days alone."

"Truly?" Her response was not what I expected. "I am curious how you persuaded the drezdarr to permit such a request."

"Oh, I didn't have to do any convincing. I asked Celeste for a favor, and she took care of the rest."

"The drezdarrina can be very persuasive." I chuckled, lowering my hands to Cara's backside.

"Yeah, though I think it has more to do with Khyron not being able to tell her no."

"And the favor you mentioned?" Khyron might not be able to resist Celeste's charm, but he was also shrewd and would expect something in return for his generosity.

"Well, I kind of volunteered us for a mission." Cara bit her lower lip.

All thoughts of enticing her back into bed vanished. I tensed, expecting the worst. "What kind of mission?"

"How does taking another trip to Golyndier sound? Since we haven't had any luck finding the ketaurran who was involved with Doyle, I thought it might be worth talking to Des and seeing if he knows anything." She entwined her fingers in the hair at my nape. "I promise I'll even take you along this time."

"That is very generous of you." Our relationship had gotten a lot stronger since our last visit to the small town. We trusted one another, and I knew she would never purposely leave me behind.

"I thought so."

"What was the other thing you needed to take care of, vrincorra?" I asked.

"First of all, I'm not a blossom with thorns." She narrowed her gaze and squirmed, trying to get away.

I tightened my grip, refusing to let her go. "Of course you are not." I brushed kisses along the skin at the base of her neck. "Would there happen to be a second of all?"

"Um, yes." She moaned.

"Which is?" I worked my way to her earlobe, then grazed it with my teeth.

"A surprise, but you'll only get it if you get back in bed."

I was an intelligent male and knew that any surprise involving my ketiorra and a bed could not be bad. I released her immediately, my eagerness making her giggle. I hopped onto the bed with my back propped against the wall, my legs stretched out in front of me. "I am ready."

"I can see that." She grinned wickedly, then began removing her pants. She wiggled more than necessary, bending over to give me a view of her partially covered backside as she slowly slid the fabric down her legs.

My erection had gotten harder, my anticipation of watching her remove the top in the same manner great. When she turned to leave the room, I groaned. "Cara, wait. Where are you going?" Being playful was one thing, torturing a male past his point of endurance was another.

"Not far." She crouched in the doorway and reached for whatever she had sitting on the floor on the opposite side of the wall. When she returned to her feet, she held a small sealed container.

She sauntered back to the bed, crawled in next to me, then straddled my lap. "Did you know that Khyron has a huge kitchen area and several females who cook for him?"

I was curious to know what was in the container, but did not see the connection between Khyron's food preparation area and me pleasuring Cara until she cried out my name. "I am aware. I have visited the area many times outside of regular meals when I was in need of something additional to eat."

"Why doesn't that surprise me?" She set the container between us, then removed the seal.

The aroma of freshly prepared pyteinnas filled the air. "Did you prepare these…for me?" It warmed me knowing she had gone to a lot of trouble to prepare my favorite food.

"I did, but I have to confess I have an ulterior motive."

"You do?" I took a bite, savoring the flavor, and waited for her to explain.

"I plan to spend several hours locked in a bathing room and wanted to make sure you have plenty of strength."

It seemed Cara's fascination with what we could do in the large stone tubs equaled my own. I looked at the layers of flat cakes and grinned. "I do not know if this will be enough."

"We'll see." Giggling, she grabbed the container, sealing it as she slid off the bed.

She was through the doorway and halfway across the gathering room before I caught up with her. I grabbed her around the waist, tossed her over my shoulder, then continued heading for the bathing room.

"Zaedon, if you don't put me down right now, I'll show you just how prickly I can be."

"That is the plan, my lovely vrincorra." I pinched her backside, enjoying the sound of her squealing laughter.

175

"That is definitely the plan."

# ABOUT THE AUTHOR

Rayna Tyler is an author of paranormal and sci-fi romance. She loves writing about strong sexy heroes and the sassy heroines who turn their lives upside down. Whether it's in outer space or in a supernatural world here on Earth, there's always a story filled with adventure.

Printed in Great Britain
by Amazon

17354445R00105